CU00944223

1 2 JUN 2015

Suffolk
County Council

Please return/renew this item
by the last date shown.

Suffolk Libraries
01473 584563
www.suffolk.gov.uk/libraries/

BRICKS

BRICKS

LEON · JENNER

CORONET

First published in Great Britain in 2011 by Coronet
An imprint of Hodder & Stoughton
An Hachette UK company

1

Copyright © Leon Jenner 2011

A CIP catalogue record for this title is available from the British Library.

ISBN 978 1 444 70628 4

Typeset in Stempel Garamond by Hewer Text UK Ltd, Edinburgh
Printed and bound by Clays Ltd, St Ives plc

Hodder & Stoughton policy is to use papers that are natural, renewable
and recyclable products and made from wood grown in sustainable
forests. The logging and manufacturing processes are expected to
conform to the environmental regulations of the country of origin.

During the writing of this book, I have lost my Nan, but gained a wife, Katherine, a son, Jack and a Bump!

This book is dedicated to all of them.

ACKNOWLEDGEMENTS

Thank you to Mark Booth and Charlotte Haycock for your belief and guidance and in refining this, my first book.

Thank you also to all at Coronet and their freelancers, in particular Stuart Bache and Jorn Kaspuhl for the beautiful cover and illustrations.

Thank you to Stephen J. Murray, whose website www. dot-domesday.me.uk is an invaluable source on early British history.

I

Amongst the red dust, standing in a solid yet temporary timber shed, I work, a practitioner of the art of red masonry. My craft, initiated by apprenticeship, is refined by experience and from absorbing the knowledge of my compatriots.

In a circular motion on a perfectly trued York stone, I rub a brick of exquisite fabric. The shed I work in is poorly lit, sacrificing the light to protect my esoteric art. I have risen to become a highly revered being: my knowledge and practice of natural philosophy, art and mathematics incarnate me as Newton and Michelangelo combined.

I am a bricklayer.

In the process of creating a niche, I embody my profession at its zenith.

Drafting the design of the niche and setting out the means to cut and shape every brick, creating an architectural jewel.

But why am I doing this? What are the motivating factors? Is it for the money?

No, there are other ways to make money, far easier ways that require less skill, knowledge and effort. Is it for the kudos? Maybe, but kudos doesn't have to combine with strained eyesight and choking dust. Is it because I was not given the choice to do anything else? This could also be so, but to reach such a level of perfection requires more than begrudging acceptance of circumstance.

I love the process of rubbing the bricks square, their texture, the crispness of their arrises as I prepare to cut them to shape. Sometimes, whilst doing this, the distant aroma of the kiln fire is released, completing the representation of the elements. Above all, when the work is finished, the excitement is breathtaking:

I have created a monument to my consciousness, made real the abstraction of my mind.

This bricklayer is mortared to the Earth by the bonds of nature. My thoughts were created by the same forces that created and fired the clay. I have raised my art to both purify and embellish this basic human need for a home. With the preparation and the laying of one brick at a time, I play out the sequence of nature's quanta, creating something complex, important and beautiful. Could this be a ritual representation of the quantum world creating the elements and in turn laying them down to create life?

These lumps of baked mud I shape and lay so lovingly are

the product of ice ages, of physics, of the fundamental forces of nature that created our universe, our planet and our higher human consciousness. All of these things, reduced and embodied in the brick.

2

Standing alone in that dark shed, with the familiarity of my work for company. The sharp earthy aroma, the trace of burning coals releasing as I cut and rub the block of fired earth, I begin to think of how I came to be, and why, out of the vastness of creation, I should come to be here and doing this. My work saves me from the despair of nothingness and idleness, my self-esteem is built by my walls, and by their creation I am validated.

Looking through a gap, I see the escarpment of the Downs. They talk of the mysterious hills as being the birthplace of Druids. I know of Druids. When pronounced correctly, the word Druid will sound like the call of an owl. From birth I have been taught the secrets of life. The greatest lesson of all is to keep those secrets secret. For, you see, the rest of you are not quite ready yet to understand the full richness and magic of life. Even though you look in awe at the wonders of nature and you are told of and shown its magnificence, something of a void emanates from within.

That void, created by the denial of instinct, stops you from fully taking in breath.

Almost conspiratorially you are stopped from thinking too deeply. But throughout the mists of time, a standard-bearer for the shift of consciousness that you daily experience, though you may not be aware of it, has worked his task efficiently. Although you are not yet ready to know the truth, you are at a crossroads. Because of this I will grant you a few secrets. When you are told some of them, you will know them to be true without any further explanation.

People like me walk amongst you now. We are the tenets of secret and powerful knowledge. We hold everything together, we know everything, we are eternal and we are driven by the form and function of beauty. You, my friend, have until now been living barely half a life. Why must you analyse and use so much reason in your life? You know the very greatest things cannot be reasoned. You know it and you feel it. Life is breath and the beating of your heart. This pulse is visible in every quantum of matter. This pulsating rhythm of breath and blood is mimicking the flicker of matter into our existence. You see, you have been made so that you can experience snippets of the true consciousness.

We flow through many dimensions, and when we flow through the ones we are meant for we become real and quantum energy ticks into existence. It is the gaps of nothingness where the real energy, the real power and real importance lie, between every quantum pulse, between every breath and heartbeat. How you experience things is caused by this pulse refracting through further dimensions, slowing and speeding up energy, creating the illusion you perceive as reality. In the past, life was rich and deep. Indeed, in some parts of the world the old consciousness lives on, under pressure, but unyielding. People were not as they look now. Well, some were, our physical ancestors. But there were other people, somewhat different.

The world back then was the highest expression of the human mind. Most of us now are dull and a poor race in comparison. The world now is dominated by science and by its methods. These methods seek the truth, but by their rigidity and narrowness of mind they steer away from the truth. The ego of science is fearful of deeper understanding and by its very nature will not find the progress it seeks. The truth does not entirely lie in the scientific method, but these days it comes remarkably close, despite the dominance of the materialist philosophy. This proximity, although limited to a few areas, is worthy of much debate. String, M-Theory and any notions of multiple dimensions or many abstract worlds, of course, meet with my approval.

Bricks

From ladders to measures, to creation of bliss
I am the tekton that proceeds over this.
The architect is nothing without the refiners of his vision
and I am that which marks with precision the datum and line,
ladders to the divine and all that is needed to realise the climb,
material creation of will,
celestial until the dawn stands still into the void of glory ever more,
towers on this world will soar but you must sustain what was my
*   domain*
or all of my noble work is in vain.
My towers will crumble,
my world stands still
and I am lost and all is in vain
as I will crumble into an abyss,
lost in all I strive for bliss unto the world and fragile void
I will not last a moment more
but with your scaffold you will shore
my dreams divine and all of your lives will shine.
Within my wall abstraction made real –
this is the right way you must not steal,
or you will turn my walls around and liberation turns within,
a fine line between prison and sin.
With all that I stand and create and love,
remember that God cannot make without us,
we are his hands, his dexterous will. But mine is to decide every
*   detail,*

Leon Jenner

and, as you know, the details make the whole, united in homogene-
   ous mass, without which would crumble and crush,
this whole world is made by us,
so follow our path or all is lost,
as all refined and thoughtful generation
is nothing without your attentive consideration.

3

The creation of matter is tied to the creation of consciousness. People in the past instinctively felt that the existence they experienced was a trapped and partial one. As I have said, there are more dimensions to existence than the ones you sense, even if some of you sense more than others.

Life is not as bland as many of you think. You must look out of yourself to realise your place and your fortune. The challenges that we suffer are the product of our way of thinking. Inside your mind, the cells that make you up have specialised to form the neuron.

We are learning a lot about our brains, but are struggling with our minds. This is because we deny our ethereal essence its rightful place.

In the past, long ago, in the north of what is now England, a tribal nation created a sacred landscape. In that landscape was a centrepiece. This centrepiece chose its own position. As

I said before, the people back then were of a higher consciousness. They knew the ways of the world, and they understood the lines of energy that circumnavigate the Earth.

This focal point in a sacred landscape, like others all over the world, attracted many, many people at the special times of year. In this particular case the monument of three circular mounds joined by a causeway was honouring a group of stars in the sky. The three henge monuments extend for over a mile and once were a brilliant gypsum white. They were a recreation of the belt of the Orion constellation as it was back then.

The Thornborough Henges, as they are now called, are under threat. The material found in the immediate landscape, gypsum, is of commercial value. The sacred landscape and the setting for the henges is being destroyed; another blood sacrifice to the economic god.

As we look up to Orion now, with our technology of telescopes, we view a dark nebula. This cloud of dust is the remains of what was once a brilliant, awesome star. In tune with the cyclical law of nature, it has now become the birthplace of stars. Inside this interstellar cloud of dust and energy, a new star will form, and from the power of the formation of that star, nuclear fusion will form compounds and molecules that will eventually create planets and the material for life. These people, when building this monument, knew where they came from.

And at that infamous monument of stones further south, Stonehenge, constant arguments arise about moving the road that passes so close to it. Amongst these squabblers, not one of them would believe that the stones were carried by ship and thoughts alone. Yes, it's true, every stone was lifted by one person who used his mind to do so, following the stone in trance and bliss. You probably don't realise that most of the stones were stood upright and concreted in position in the twentieth century. This is also true.

We, however, are not born in the way you would expect. I am just a normal human being, I wasn't born until I had been here for over thirty years, but throughout the time of my conception I received much preparation. It took a great pain in my life, a pain that ran so deep it cut into the places between heartbeats. With this I died. And when I died they took me to the axis. This is the first place, the place where all of the matter and energy originate. Unfortunately I cannot describe it to you. Your minds are such now that it would be like explaining light to a blind man.

4

Julius Caesar was not in search of mere material gain when he tried twice to invade Britain. The Roman historian Suetonius stated that Caesar was in search of pearls. These were metaphorical pearls of wisdom.

He did not have the power to act alone. One of my kind saw him as a suitable vessel with which to reshape your belief of reality. True power does not present itself. This is an important rule. When I think of the one who manipulated Caesar, or rather those who manipulated him, I don't think of them as evil. You see, all of our kind share the same knowledge, and how we interpret that knowledge is up to us, and as we are the masters and mistresses of this domain our wisdom is our only regulator. But as we the wise use our wisdom, our wisdom in turn may use us.

Things have changed with ferocious rapidity of late; the world has changed so much. Although I am a citizen of the world and knew of a time when the world had one language, far beyond speech, that united it, I now choose to live in a sacred part of England. There is great power and importance to this physical particular place, and I need to be here. I have been here before, when the magic was more obvious.

Britain was a magical land. The air was sweet, the essence of life shone through the Sun on to 3,000-year-old oaks. They would say that they were the giant daughters of deities and men. Skylarks, eagles, wolves: a richness of life like a symphony, and every view a panorama of dreamy beauty and bliss, enriched by a noble and magnificent people. I used to wander through the landscape, so powerful yet delicate, evoking all the ages of time as one instant and unifying you to all you feel and see. Walking along wide oak slab roads, through expansive magical marsh, through a forest of reeds and up into the chalk hills on to pathways of dusty white stone. You would frequently see travellers of all kinds on chariot, horse, wagon or on foot. Magnificent carvings of spirits adorned the hills, icons to show that you were in the nation of these people. On your travels you could rest at the powerful circular lodges. These replenished body and spirit. The Sun and sky, forest and field embraced you, protected you: a sanctuary, an eternal garden, a paradise. I remember the time clearly.

Sensing the coming of the Roman mindset, I drew together the local kings. We met in a meeting house built for the sole purpose of this discussion.

'The time has come for the union of our two kinds to end.'

That opening line drew silence. For ten thousand years we had lived with these people. We were in symbiosis with them. A selected few would give us our physical bodies and we would hold their society together in exchange for making us, the shapeless, into the real. Many trained for the task from before the time they could walk, but few proved to be able to accept or comprehend the meaning of our ways.

These people were newcomers to us. Through them we have stimulated the potential of humanity. We exist as consciousness. You exist in these many realms at once, and we try to balance you so that your time here follows the correct path. Most of the time these days you won't hear us. We whisper to you through a powerful invention of ours, emotions. We use emotions and tie them to colours. Everything has an emotion and a colour, every taste, everything you look at or hear or feel. That is all there is to communication. Emotion and colour.

You used to be able to harness this power, and indeed you still can if you have the courage. Try speaking to a plant next time you are on your own, but speak only with colour and emotion. It will work, believe me. The plant is much smarter than you.

When you learn how, you can extend your voice to communicate to anything in the universe, past and present. If you are having a problem understanding this, try to think back. When you were small, you associated a colour with a day of the week or a smell or even a number. This may go with shapes and images. The power is there inside you. I bet that sometimes when you look at a landscape, you draw intersecting lines with your mind and map out the land. See how much you have and how little you use? Time is also a creation to help with your perception, just as big an illusion as reality. Just remember that everything in your entire life is from your dialogue with emotion, it really is as simple as that.

The problem with this simplicity is that just a subtle disruption can disturb the balance. As a stone thrown into a pond creates ripples. The rippling of equilibrium of emotional communication can stretch throughout generations. Subtle disruptions can enslave nations and create wars.

Back on the islands of Britain and throughout the world at that time we could stop a war by simply walking alone between the two armies seconds before a crucial battle. As they began to charge, we would walk between them and they would stop. By the evening they would be feasting together as brothers and sisters. Sometimes it was our strategy to get them to this point and then stop them at the final moment before conflict. This helped emphasise the stupidity of their arguments. If the battle had occurred, their minds would have darkened, disturbing the balance of emotions.

This part of the world was one of the places we could most effectively communicate with people. The scientists and historians now call these people the Celts, but this thinking comes from the prejudiced viewpoint of those who must find physical evidence before they can think. These were people of many names and fashions. Of rich variety and subtlety. These 'Celts' were some of the last enlightened people in the area. Although they had kings and queens, they were ruled by a unifying heart. It is so hard for me to communicate the reality of the past to you because I am relying on words that have their source among the conquerors of these people. Yes, I know of the Germanic, French and other roots of the English language, but they are spoken now firmly in the context of the Roman mindset. Thinking back again to that meeting with the British kings, it would be over one hundred years before our ways began to part. But for a people who honoured their ancestors from ten thousand years before and beyond, they acknowledged that they must now make preparations. I knew that one of my kind had created this Roman consciousness and it had swept northwards towards us. Its power was in its incompatibility with the older ways of thinking.

They broke the old laws. I pitied Caesar, a mere puppet. He once wept because he hadn't conquered the world by the age of thirty. Dictators in waiting at that time aspired to Alexander. Men like Caesar did not know how he achieved his aims. They also went on to find out the true cost of such consummated ambition.

5

Everyone must reconcile themselves to their sins. Sin is a term taken from archery; it simply means to miss the mark. You cannot ever truly be judged as good or evil. Your actions are the result of your interpretation of emotion. You are communicated the correct path always. If you miss, and some miss very badly indeed, then you must make amends. If you kill, then you must share the required amendments with your victim. If you kill over a million, as Caesar said he did, then you will be toiling for some time. And if you kill or harm a child, you are at the mercy of generations of their ancestors. These rules apply to us; that's why we make use of people like Caesar, for they take the bulk of sin.

At times it must seem that there is great evil. We hear stories of terrifying, gruesome acts, but these are the results of our links to emotions being twisted by our own cognitive poisons. This can occur from generation to generation. It is up to you, if you are such a person able to commit such an act, to break this cycle. If you have suffered as a child, you should know all the more the suffering you inflict and the cycle you perpetuate. You must bear the light out of the darkness of your family.

You have chosen your challenges in life. You chose them, believe it or not, before you were born. It may surprise you that, despite what you think, you chose your own parents. You chose the challenges you live because you are strong enough to meet them. It is because you have lost sight of the path behind you that you sometimes feel so weak. In the past, people could remember back to a time before they were born. To remember back this far is to know your true name. You are capable of this; you must try it.

Deep down you will know this to be true. Deny the dogma and the illusions that surround you and be brave enough to face yourself. When it comes to others' opinions, especially the ones who think they have a higher purpose in life because they have sat a few exams, remember this Latin phrase: '*nullius in verba*', take nobody's word for it. I am not particularly keen on the Romans, as you can imagine, but using the occasional Latin phrase makes me sound so much more sophisticated. Besides, that one I just used is a good one.

You may be wondering now why I started by stating that I was a bricklayer. Well, you see, the home is a representation of our soul. When we dream of a house or our home we are seeing our soul, or even, sometimes, the soul of another.

Therefore, throughout the ages, we the druids have been drawn to the notion of building. You see, our physical environment is more important to us than we dare imagine. An individual home, right through to entire cities and nations, must be well built.

The design of these buildings and wider expanses is the easy part. It is the spirit in which a house is built that is of the real importance. How you feel as you lay each brick is absorbed into the fabric of the home. Only the one who works with their hands can transmit this love into every minute detail of the fabric of a building. They will touch every tiny part of your house, the physical representation of your soul. Only they will see every detail and influence that detail. This applies not only to every brick, but to every nail and fixing of everything. An unhappy builder can have a dramatic effect on a building, even if it looks perfect on the outside and inside. Remember, the gaps between the heartbeats are the most important, the most powerful.

6

I remember standing on the shore over gleaming white cliffs – no, not Dover, further to the west in an area more sacred. This whiteness earned this land its name. Albion, the white land. The currents across the Channel brought you here from the continent. This place was closer in time by these currents, although not by distance; the will of the sea to bring you here could not be forced by geometry.

Appearing over the horizon, a massive fleet of ships ebbed towards us. They raced ahead of the rising light of the sun as the sea began to sparkle. I saw in the minds of the veterans their fear of our barbarous nature, our mysterious violence.

The Romans quivered, hiding their fears behind ashen faces, some torn between their instincts and loyalty to their fortune-blessed commander. Some of the Romans jumped overboard; suicide now, they thought: surely the sea is more merciful.

Stories of the past year filled the ranks and spread fear to all. The terror and loneliness. It is as if your gods have left you, the cries around echoing from the depths of the undergrowth. Some of them, the Romans, were left to dangle in the trees. How a breathless corpse cries louder than the living.

So many of them spent their time panting and panicking, fumbling amongst the alien soil.

They believed they pushed ahead when in fact they were being pushed.

At the shore we prepared banners and silks. I watched the magnificence of the Britons and their exotic adornment of no more than woad and ochre, gold and jewel eyes. Horns rallied chariots, vibrant in colour and energy. The chariots moved to the edge of the cliff, and with them effigies of giants, adorned with flowing bright silks, giving the appearance of life in the breeze. There were giants here once, but that is another story.

Caesar stood at the bow of his ship. The ship he chose was new – no patched-up hull or rapid repair.

His brown eyes were fixed on our coast. Others turned to pray, eyes up and palms asunder, waiting to receive good grace. 'Our fight is with the people of this land, dear gods, not with you.' Little did they understand.

On the shore we were prepared, all landing places covered and connected to us with our deep bonds to the land. Such places were but an extension of the warrior deities that guarded them, with their swords and shields, their pounding hearts, the energy of the breath of every horse and man, woman and child condensing into the air and joining with the heavens as a smoke stack rising to the infinite universe.

Caesar drew upon the shore. Clumsiness again. The ships rocked and fumbled, clattering into the shingle. The rest of the fleet lay in a wide and distant arc behind, the Romans afraid to leave the bosom of their ships. Before them a great estuary of tranquil peace.

The ships began to land along the coast. The Romans uttered war cries as they mustered the courage to disembark. Their customary silence would have signalled their confidence, so this insecure roar comforted me.

They spilled forth from the ships, their armour gleaming and faces shaved clean as if every stroke of razor and cloth could wipe away forlorn anxiety. A clutter and jangle on to the snapping, hailing crunch of the shingle, rivers of men forming into columns and mass, a machine whose parts were made of fleshy entities.

At this spectacle the British kings looked on, these leaders chosen by ballot from the will of their tribes for their deep courage and noble pride; a tear ran from my eye as I felt their envy of Caesar's power, the control of his men and mastery of their valour. I myself longed for the power to stop their advance.

The British kings were quickly brought round and cried out the order, to crush the tin men, if possible singling out the traitors from Gaul, twice the stature of the men from Rome, for a more time-consuming death.

Rocks from the shore rained down, mixed with arrows flowing like a shower of deadly serpents, striking with a hunter's instinct. Clattering, screaming, crying to the maternal goddess. Muffled throes of death as throats crushed and sinews tore, the thick smell of blood filled the air so that it was iron to taste, and the breakers of the sea strove to wash the pebbles clean with its equally salty lick.

With every death, he or she who loosed it would own the soul as a slave. The Britons, seeing the souls of the Romans by their mortal incarnations, sought to claim them as bounty. The soul of the horse would pull their chariots, the soul of the man multiply their strength and speed, as if with every strike of his fist his captive souls would strike in unison. The slain only become free when their new master dies. If they knew this, surely they wouldn't have come?

But Caesar arrogantly saw this place as Gaul. He sought to find the strifes and superstitions of the people and turn them where it would most advantage him. These islands of Britain were isolated from the work that had gone on thousands of years before in Gaul. Already there it was weakened, cracks appeared in the soul of the place, as if to give momentum to this day.

As the Romans advanced through the loosely wooded estuary, our chariots raced as boulders down the slopes. They moved as if gliding, pulled by a pair of fine horses, controlled by two warriors. The rider as an acrobat, standing with a foot on either horse, the other throwing javelins that never missed. I knew the Romans would see this as a foolish tactic, to race down from the advantage of high ground, but they could not understand the superior horsemanship of my friends, the speed at which they turned and vanished back up the hill after inflicting their wrath.

The Romans were unaware that the chariots were as numerous as stars, behind the deep dark trees and up the slopes. Sent only a few at a time to race down the hill, and returning to be passed by fresh and eager warriors, all the time a constant battery.

From their world to ours, theirs so shallow and ours so deep, they couldn't respond to our attack. At first Caesar had seen our armies as arcane, like the Greeks many years before. He saw our ways as backward, but now he began to learn. As his army began to break up, our plan was failing, not because of our struggle, but his.

I saw into Caesar's mind and sensed his fear, I found his plan and at once sought to seize upon it. I advised the counter to it. First we needed to lure them deeper, so we could swallow them whole, dissolve them in time. They would vanish and so would their wants.

We withdrew and melted into the forest as quickly as the Sun behind a cloud. A few moments of silence and then slowly the return of nature's chatter, a few moments more and the Romans began to roar with the arrogant sense of victory. Only one young solider, seeing no bodies of the enemy, couldn't understand the retreat.

They continued to march inland, not too far from the river that fed the estuary they landed on. Turning into winding deep and sunken roads, the tracks left behind by vast herds of red deer over millennia, deep into the inland forests of the north.

The columns of men trundled along these paths, their cavalry through the woods above, protecting the baggage and seeking a place to make a camp. I sat high in the trees with a party of warriors and we watched as they arrogantly trudged by. As numerous as the oaks, never had this place seen so many men gathered. I caught sight of a large horseman, a Gaul no doubt because of his stature, and nodded forward my head. In an instant an arrow pierced his cheek, he screamed and fell from his horse and the tired Romans disarrayed, trying to act as if on an open field, to reform in a regular way. Swords drawn and casting their eyes all around, they saw every fifth tree loose a hail of arrows, tips with flint and iron, bursting through shield and armour, the screams of men resounding, the clattering of metals and neighing, bucking horses. Those shouting commands for order were brought down and pierced.

As quickly as we came, we left. They groaned and stumbled on their way, not so confident of quick victory now, but with the belief that we were a desperate haranguing foe and that they would soon establish their eagle. On they went and found a clearing.

We let them build their fort. An ugliness skewed the structure, made partly from the trees of our land and partly as a kit brought from Gaul. It pierced our land in a place forbidden and without asking who needed to be asked. The act of building this encampment was indeed an insult too far and the whole land, even the sky and sea around for countless miles, responded with a quiet anger. However, we let them build their prison.

Its wooden walls and ditches stood solidly, but those inside wondered which way the walls truly faced. Its squared form betrayed it as a trespasser. All around we observed and listened. We waited for action, occasionally taking down a sentry. When it was decided to send out scouts, we made sure they never returned. Eventually and gradually we eased off so their confidence grew. As their supplies ran low, foraging and hunting parties had to be sent out. We watched and let them gather and kill. They had no knowledge of these islands' botany and of our mastery of it, of our genius.

We sowed a poison all around that would be consumed by the boar, by the fowl and fox, the bear and squirrel. No harm would come of these creatures; they would not know they had been poisoned, for we could mark our poison, name it to a race, a tribe, a single soul. This is a common trick in our warfare, and the antidote is secret and not what you would expect. Without this antidote, if you feast on the flesh of the poisoned, the toxins will come alive with the power of the animal you ate. Its soul will attack you from within; every cell will be seized and clawed at. You would die in thirty days. The ensuing dysentery, the dissolving of brain and kidney, eyeball, tongue and skin finished them.

We waited, now in full view of the fort. We quietly watched, listened and heard the odd lonely splutter break the silence from within. It took only several days for the acrid, poisonous smell of death to fill the place where once confident and proud men lived with the minutiae of duty. We loosed a hail of burning arrows to cleanse the place.

As the crackle quickened and the cinders rose, the door of the fort opened. Out burst the general Caesar, escaping from his rotting, festering army with a small band of guards.

A dark humour filled us as they vomited whilst trying to stay on the backs of their horses, bloody liquid excrement smeared down their thighs and the flanks of the beasts they could barely ride. Some fell and were killed in an instant by their weakened state. The ones who, despite the damage to their minds, could still muster up innovation, had tied themselves to their horse. They bounced around like corpses as the horses galloped. To us the macabre rush wrought a comic rapture.

I stood at the interface of two parallel worlds. At the cusp of a possible change, beyond all reason or knowledge, to those who would fight for it or against it. Those who would fight for things to remain the same or for the change that would alter human history, alter the mind of every man and woman and of every life on this Earth.

When the ships appeared they marked the moment of the watershed, the changing of a consciousness of geological power. Mankind's brief term was all-encompassing and dominant over the world, but on the whole he lived with the rhyme of nature and the soul of the Earth, knowing the spheres where all things operated, having the understanding that time, in its gentleness, could not be bought or forced faster. But this new consciousness wanted to smash such things and, with an arrogant greed, command nature's rhythms and bend them to their will. Their blind ego was such that they believed they were the first of all people and the harnessers of the gods' will. They believed that they were above all that was truly above them and they sought to destroy anything that might confront their self-perception. From art to logic and from shore to shore, their short-term lusts multiplied into millennia of change. They would unconsciously preside over the rise of money, the creation of polar economics, where some had all and most had none. And with this lust for conquest they would seduce and burn where necessary. They would alter all for their benefit, and for their benefit all would alter.

Staring over stormy seas awaiting furthermore
The riches of another world more worthless than the poor
Who need the bones of noble men for altars to adore
Upon their crimson purple robes the blood hides in the seams
casting a shadow distant more than the tallest trees
A broken truth they follow with their ugly greed
That stems from vanity and dark and lonely need
They sailed towards the world's end; not knowing it was the
     beginning
They tried to crush a lasting light that shone with love and singing
A resonant note that held in place our place in nature's destiny
That sang and sang and soothed all men in times of trying ecstasy
That hid the lies and drove the wise into the truth so effortlessly
Now smothered in lies and tricked by wise and wrong-minded
     thoughts of the thoughtless.
They sailed closer like a tidal wave to smother,
break and wipe clean millennia of understanding of all the world's
     needs
But to them the time was wrong and this I knew instinctively
That they would lose and make their noose among this misty
     destiny
For the past is hidden from you. Know again of what you once were
But the people of these islands' blood runs through you far and far
They fight on in you and lost in many worlds
And polarised your mind, hiding in the furls
of all that life is meant to be, what's right is hidden materially

Bricks

But truth is lasting yet following the laws of entropy,
never dying, merely fleeting, from place to place eternally.
They neared the beach, the nagging boats neighing with bold
*   ferocity*
The sea it broiled by my thoughts but the spell was cast half in vain
as the chiefs' and queens' eyes glinted at the fame, the charisma,
the mastery of the game
The brave and painted woaded men and women from afar,
within the deep and misty land crashed into the wandering star,
and with their boldened fight of rushing conflicting energy.
The clashing of sword and slicing flesh, returning similar infamy.
But then the break, to lead them through into the deeper land
To swallow, digest and spit back over the waters.
But all in vain as queen and chief wanted round to turn to square,
within this fold even though it was their lair.
The seduction of such control, of men who wouldn't argue.
But would bend to your only will and die on your word.
And with your word would thrust a thousand swords,
what great power and as such adored.
The edge was lost from this valiant deed,
of fighting for long-term forlorn seed
To sow into the minds of men to stop them ever changing,
and stem the world of deadly Roman weeds.
That would sink deep into the meadows of your mind,
suppressing tender flowers,
uprooting them from your psyche,

tearing you from your roots so that you would tumble aimlessly.
Yet knowing deep down that there is more than this,
you try to root in vain and cling to impostors' mist.
But into the depths of this land the clockwork Rome progressed,
slashing through the green and gold embracing earthly twists,
of valley field on lonely trail unwalked on ever by men.
They cut through the delicate air like an arrow through a cloud.
And all the gods mourned the birth of their antithesis.
But I knew the truth and knew I must defend it,
for I led them on and watched them build their edifice.
Of beautiful noble oak they slashed and squared and righted,
into an impregnable fort,
defended strong, and mighted
by the robot men who thoughts were not their own.
They knew nothing of this Earth but for their faces etched in
    muddy stone.
And their dented, tarnished armour against the whispering trees.
Unheard by them, this nature was oblivious to what they perceive.
As stars die and the universe flies, the birds dodge the bees.
How could they know that for nobility they were only thieves?
As they feasted on our fauna we cracked a wicked grin,
for we knew that we had turned their walls and imprisoned them
    from within.
The game you see on which they feasted greedily,
was permeated by our infinite knowledge of this island's botany.
As we watched them die and saw the clouds of mistletoe smoke,

to drive the flies, the fear from their eyes satisfying our cruel joke.
It was our wont to smother them in disease and then with fire,
and let the branches of our forest soak them up forever.
They weren't the first, nor would they be the last,
many have disappeared into this secret vast.
The truth was hidden from the people of the enemy,
but further mistake was for this time to send back a story,
of how invaders die in the seduction of their glory.
We let the man who led them gallop in the wind,
forever disabled by our secret gin,
we let him ride unto an unmolested ship,
and set them sail, sent them on the wind,
to learn that such folly should never be tried again.
But as we had poisoned, he had poisoned us,
his wild and ugly spore had fallen on the ground.
Leaving a trail foolishly welcoming next time around.

7

Caesar's fortune was bestowed upon him by his deal with his helpers. But the poison affected him throughout the remainder of his life. Our revenge would resurface as unpredictable seizures. He would later orchestrate his own death so that he would remain noble. Ingraining him into the Roman version of history. How foolish they were to set foot in a land that was mapped out in a way they could not comprehend.

Yet this system is so simple if you know how. The traces of this mapping can still be found around you. The directions of old roads and their intersecting points guarding the energy of these places. This system works through time, so these energy points are fluid and forever changing. This applies to everywhere in the world but especially to this venerable pole. A journey can only be made when the road is ready to take you. And you can only vanquish an enemy by understanding the land, its energy and its cycles.

And so for a while the calm returned. And this seat of learning remained in our hands. This archipelago was the core of our being and the place where our art was learnt at its best. This magic, which could not be viewed by sight, blew over the land. It is still there, you can see it if you look hard enough. If you look at a tree or any plant you will see a leaf moving in a way that is different from the rest; it will shake itself at you or wave out of rhythm with other leaves blowing in the wind. Naturally some will state that this is the product of vortexes, but it is not this alone. Would this leaf still signal to you if you were not there to see it? No, it would not.

I will tell you now about my earlier life. I remember a childhood reasonably happy. I was fascinated by the workings of the world, by science, nature, energy, time and space. Long blissful summers and cool embracing winters. But then, at about the age of twelve, a sea of blackness began to envelop me. At one point, as a boy of fourteen, lying alone in bed, the pain and horror of every spirit entered me. I could see the agony of grief in every living soul. Injustice, anger and pain screamed into me. The pain was so severe that I couldn't weep or speak or feel. It surrounded me and absorbed me. No light entered my life any more, except at rare moments. These brief occasions of joy served to further amplify the pain by their contrast. I was also kept out of reach of the things I truly needed. I wanted to create and wonder, but my enemies denied me this also. Misery, which can only be described as an endless hollow scream, stopped me from using the subtleties of emotion.

The symptoms were invisible to others and as a result I was forced to add guilt to my pain. The crushing brought about the need to escape, to die. It seemed there was no resolving it because there seemed no beginning or end to it. Still this pain stayed with me as I grew older and the symptoms remained hidden.

Everyone told me how charismatic, how handsome, how intelligent I was. The world was at my feet, they would say. But this means nothing. It was as if tears flowed down the inside of my face, invisible to all but me. Your inner world is all you truly have, and if you can, learn to create it to its full potential. Only then may you master true happiness. The exterior world mirrors this internal world, so every thought is a prayer.

But in me the howling, screaming wind persisted. I set myself a goal. Be happy by thirty-three or leave this world and this body. Throughout that time there were women who came and went, taking and giving me something each time. I struggled with businesses and jobs. Trying to be free and find happiness, I threw myself into my work, but all I felt was drudgery and misery. I did not seek solace in material things like most. I aspired to discipline and order, trying to train myself as a citizen monk. I followed the philosophies of the greats, both ancient and modern, yet their words drew hollow breath. Occasionally I could cry, bringing such sweet relief, but at the same time this relief released my motivation enough to commit the darkest solitary act.

On one of these weeping occasions, at the age of thirty-three, I chose death. Standing in the middle of my front room, in my damp and tiny cave of an apartment, I sought out in my mind the best way to die. Walking over to the drawer in the kitchenette, I slid it open and selected a carving knife. The blade was about seven inches long. I took the knife and, with my rudimentary knowledge of anatomy, I placed the point of the blade below my breastbone, angled it upwards towards my heart. I had prayed many times for this heart to stop beating, but it wouldn't. I used to punch my chest and scream and beg, and when I could, I would weep. But it kept beating, kept living, kept pumping pain from the cosmos. But my heart wouldn't beat me this time. I would use my mind and its ultimate control over my actions to finish it. I prepared to push the knife, screwed up my eyes, held my breath with every sinew in my arms under tension. This tautness served as a controlling resistance as the tip of the blade, placed on its target between the buttons of my shirt, cut into my skin. I couldn't believe the pain from such a tiny initial wound, but I carried on.

Suddenly an operatic wave of sound pounded into my home and right through me. A female voice, the mother of life, splitting my head, she screamed like the trumpet of end times riding the top of a mile-high tsunami of sound. She forced me to drop the knife and cover my ears as I fell to my knees and cried out in pain and fear.

My heart somehow shocked into a different rhythm now. Deeper, smoother, soothing and rich, pushing a rich honey through my veins. My arms, legs, chest – every thread of my being, stripped and rebuilt. The honey filled me with a love I had long forgotten. A sublime warm feeling from early child-hood. I was soothed and the parts of me that exist between heartbeats were destroyed and remade. At this time I reached out instinctively and a hand grabbed my forearm through a psychological mist. The grip was firm yet soft. Strangely to me at the time, the hand was mine, and in its gripping grasp an overwhelming passion surged into me as every emotion sang in its highest form, lifting me. I dived into a brilliance of colour. My heart, once my eternal enemy, now flew like a dove from my chest and freed me. My rebirth was complete and now I was powerful, free and wise.

You see, since the old teaching schools were destroyed and lost forever, which I can assure you they were, we are now found and taught by our surroundings. You see, the very best teacher is within. If you listen to yourself and your surround-ings, you will be a good student, then a master soon enough. A plant will tell you if it is safe to eat it. Listen properly and it will tell you its deep history and all of its uses. Even a simple stick lying on the ground will tell you the direction you need to go in. I'm sure you are not naive enough to think they actually talk to you, like voices in your head. They communicate to you, of course, through the subtle power of emotion.

Because of the loss of the schools and the structure of the past teachings – which I assure you were not institutions, as we detest and loathe institutions; a number amongst you have played on your instinctive knowledge of us and declared themselves shamans or gurus or enlightened in some way. Even the most credible are impostors, either to themselves, to you or both. You do not have a spirit guide from an ancient Native American tribe, especially if one of your more recent ancestors was responsible for the mindless oppression and slaughter of his people. You will not get voices in your head. Unless you and your twisted interpretation of emotion make these.

Emotion is the only true medium of communication. That is all you need to know, and it is not to be mistaken for the hopelessly crude interpretation of emotion that is taught to you by the men (usually) with letters after their names. Remember, we detest and loathe institutions and the people who make them are a stain on reality, the kind of stain that causes wars and ignorance and mass murder. At their most benign they are responsible for paralysing depression and for creating the voids you feel inside. They are a tool of the others.

We are amongst you and around you. We are not necessarily entirely meek. We do not see pride as a wrong. But we are always builders. Just look at any faith and there will be a reference to a divine creator making mankind out of clay. The material of bricks, mouldable and plastic until fired hard by the brickmaker and laid by the bricklayer to create that seat of consciousness, the home. We play out this analogy in life and we are bound to our important work. We are always builders, but not all builders are us. Remember the lesson about institutions. We are not restricted to building in brick of course. Brickwork is the most symbolic of our work and will spellbind you if laid by a master.

I draw you now to the way that some very prominent institutions have had a profound effect on some of you. They make up half or so of you in number, but their importance and divinity is exponentially uncountable. They are the females amongst you. If you are a woman absorbing this text, I want you to understand that every species evolves a certain way, purely as the female chooses. Women, you may on average stand shorter than men, but the shadow you cast fades into the distance.

The differences between the sexes compensated each other and were celebrated. But deep down, and maybe by the actions of some of my colleagues who think differently from me, men began to notice that the most powerful force in life was more powerful in the women. I sigh when I see women weakening themselves and feeling insecure and unwanted.

Women are mistresses of this most powerful of forces. Sex. You spellbind men from your age of fruition. You embody the goddess creator who made this first world one-third man and two-thirds women. In order to maintain her wisdom, she would hold sway with her sexual power over the men. She could subdue the most fierce and violent, with the softness of her breast and voice and the depth of her eyes. From a fight in a pub, to the clash of civilisations, there has always been a woman who in some way acts as a catalyst or a peacemaker. So please realise your power and take it back. Your power runs deeper, greater and stronger than any ideal of feminism. You know that the world would be such a wonderful place if you were in charge again. You have the power of precedent behind you. When archaeologists around the world stop finding figurines of the universal Earth goddess, they find weapons in those upper layers of Earth.

The knowledge that was obtained to make these weapons, indeed for all of the technological shifts in humankind, was caused by a few nudges from us. I must emphasise again that we do not all share the same viewpoint. I must also emphasise that writing is a creation of one of these technological shifts and in my opinion is stifling, primitive and goes absolutely no way towards communicating the contents of my mind to yours. We never used to write anything down, and neither did you. This does not mean that we had no language. We spoke, but in more ways than I can fully explain by stringing these damned letters in a direction that doesn't seem right even to me.

Consciousness is so liquid it cannot be set in stone or letter. I must admit that it can leave you with a signature of thoughts. But this is likened to looking at the fossilised remains of an ancient beast and trying to imagine what it sounded and smelt like. Writing, although it can be from the heart, is very much a product of the head.

The brain is really the servant of the heart. I will now tell you how you came to exist. Remember I cannot tell you everything because of the primitive nature of this medium of communication, stifling further your consciousness. It is ironic, however, that consciousness is all you are. Some have stated that every piece of matter could possibly have consciousness. Very close. Every thing is consciousness. This ether-like force existed in a place that is indescribable and unimaginable. At one point there was a cataclysm and it was scattered.

Some of it was changed and moved to a different plane. Remember that this happened in a way inconceivable to you and there was no such thing as time. (You see now the problem with words!) This energy, this consciousness, by its very nature must survive and do all it can as it shifts towards its final state. It tried desperately to find its way back to the place before the cataclysm. So it began to create a place where it will start to form in a way that suited its new context. It created dimensions to move between and then it began to hum. The hum can only be perceived as a spark of sound from the perspective of each dimension, like standing at the junction of a road and seeing a car speed by. This is why physicists perceive this quantum pulse. It is all we are developed to see of this hum.

The hum twisted the shape of the dimensions so that it was

refracted in a myriad of ways. It was then that consciousness began to aggregate. It formed mass and matter and also the means for this energy to communicate. It went on to create the stellar universe and then the Earth and its counterparts. And on these planets the aggregation continued to create water and the biological molecules. These, entwined in unison, aggregated and focused the power of consciousness into cells; combinations of cells; and that most important aggregation and focuser of consciousness, the neuron. This is why you are conscious in the way you perceive. This is why you are also an incredibly rare, rich interfusion of stardust. You feel so separate from all that is around you, but you are not. The universe is your womb. You come from it and you form it. When you stare at the stars, you stare into your own mind. We chose to evolve you in a certain way so that consciousness will eventually find its way back. Some of my colleagues have interfered in this process and have made you arrogant. The destruction you wreak on the planet in the form of pollution is bad enough, as you know. But it is the harm to others that are as conscious as you that will truly bring you great retribution. Those of you that allow or inflict injustice and pain on any creature will pay immeasurably. Those of you who hide behind scientific or political methods to justify this will pay more so.

Don't hide behind economic reasons either. You know damned well what is wrong and right; if you choose wrongly you insult your ancestors and you curse the Earth. You can think of your consciousness as being like the hydrogen bond. The hydrogen bond's strength is in its weakness. It ties together with enough force to create stability, but can break easily enough to create fluidity. This bond is why water is so magical. We act like the hydrogen bonds of humanity.

The problem with the current situation is free will. Because you are free to interpret your own communication with emotion, you now do not communicate effectively with the truth and the light of your bonding with us. This though, as I have said on numerous occasions, is the manipulation of you over many generations by some of the others amongst us.

8

Julius Caesar succeeded in two ways. He set the precedent for future Roman emperors, all of whom received the same help. And he sparked envious thoughts of control and power over men and resources in the minds of the tribal kings. These two came together and formed the basis of divide and conquer. These islands were so important to capture, because from them the world could be conquered. Remember our patience. The British Empire did not have its basis entirely in greed. Because it stemmed from these islands, from a vast sacred landscape now consumed by an urban flood, some goodness entered into the mix. So, through the bad, good also came.

The world is still greatly influenced by us from these islands. The evidence for this is in the creativity that emanates from them. Remember, true power hides. When you feel low or depressed or down in any way, think of what is going on right now. Stars are being destroyed and born. The cycle of life and death continues, people are crying with grief and pain, usually far worse than yours.

Try to tap into the incredible power of all of those people in the world that are right now making love. Depression is caused by stifled anger. We all have our purpose and you have yours. There is something you are really good at and there will be a demand for what you can do. This is a law. Think outside yourself, turn away, and leave behind people who make you unhappy. People can take away your daily power but they can only take what you give. Under all circumstances, never do anything under the banner of 'I should'. You must always act on the great wisdom you are bestowed with. Remember to find emotion, see and hear it. Above all, art can cure you. And art that has its basis in the formation of a building is the most divine. The creation of a piece of art is more important than the created piece. The building process of a house is the key to the feeling of a home. Such a piece of art that could form this spiritual exercise could be in the form of an arch.

Take the time one day to build an arch. Unfortunately considered a Roman invention by some (the Romans invented nothing), the arch is the most important development in the creation of space. The span of the arch enables you to make a giant hole in a wall, without the wall collapsing, using gravity to defy gravity. Use the building of the arch as a ritual to obtain your connection to the truth. The arch and the constructing of an arch is a powerful symbol. There are many types of arch, so I will show you how to build the simplest or true arch. All of the divine buildings work in units of sixteen inches. This is an ancient and holy measurement. It is still echoed today on many modern tape measures. If you look closely, you will see a dot every sixteen inches. This measurement was used to centre joists and rafters and work out all of the critical dimensions of a building. Thus, when you build your arch, do it to span a width of at least thirty-two inches, and always in increments of sixteen inches.

A semicircular support called a centre must first be constructed, usually out of timber. This can be made by cutting out two semicircles from plywood or similar kind of board. To form the curve, you can make a trammel from a straight piece of wood. Hammer two nails at a distance exactly half of the span of the arch. The points of the nails must be at the correct distance, so take time over this. Use the trammel to draw a circle or semicircle on the ply (depending on the size of your arch) and then carefully cut out the semicircular templates. Fix these templates apart, at the width of the bricks you are using. Use good handmade stock bricks, preferably in imperial size.

Mix your mortar like this: take good lime putty, take good local building sand (it must be washed), grind up some of your bricks to a fine dust. Mix one part lime putty to two parts sand and one part brick dust. Turn your arch with care and lay the bricks from one side at a time. Keep it true and plumb and square. The extrados or outside edge should joint at no more than half an inch and no joint should intersect the centre; this should be the centre of a brick. This is the key to the perfect arch. Use common sense and intuition to fill in the gaps. Every action must be undertaken with time, precision and passion or the project will not reach its desired goals.

All of the rituals carried out in the construction of every building and every piece of a building must be performed with the correct spirit of mind. This does not involve silly dances or acts or sayings. A ritual is simply doing something with a clear, focused and true mind, and if you built your arch well you will have achieved more than any practitioner of meditation.

By building you create your consciousness and manifest your mind. When you lay each brick you should focus on that brick, using it to repel negativity. Just as the arch channels the weight of the heavens into the ground, it will channel the weight of your mind and bury it deep to the core of the Earth.

We are there, always, trying to communicate with you. I wish you would realise how much you were loved and cherished. I suppose you are wondering why we do this, why we are here. You see, without you we are incomplete. We spilled into this void with you and we need each other to get back. Just as the creation of our masterpiece is as important – or more so – than the finished product, our journey must be held to the same principles as the way we build. You come from a select few. Your ancestors stem from the few survivors of giant volcanoes, meteors, floods, pestilence, war and famine. Many times you have been refined down to a few thousand survivors around the world.

When you are feeling unlucky in your life, remember you are
not. To have got this far you are incredibly fortunate. Chance,
if you choose to call it that, has weighed in your favour. But
beware of hubris, for this is the scent irresistible to Nemesis.
Because of your ability to control your environment in such a
sudden and chaotic way, you must be whittled down occasionally. This concept applies to all of nature. One such people in
the world who are familiar with this are a people close to my
heart. The indigenous peoples around the world. I speak to
your elders directly. You must hold on to the traditions, for the
time will come when all of your children will need to know
your secrets. I know that you know this; I hope this reminder
will reinforce your faith. As the people of the nations of ancient
Australia know, those nations that live in the dry areas, you
must control the time of the fires or they will control you.

A fire is soon to come and cleanse the land. Because you
have free will, you should be prepared to reduce the great fire
that is coming. But you won't.

You worship the economic god; and although his priests,
economists, are beginning to see the importance of environment, the economic god is and always will be flawed. You have
lost the ability to measure what is important and what is truly
for the best. In your struggle you must remember that your life
is like a quantum flicker slowed down in your perception. What
is good for the economy is bad for the individual.

Like the flickering of an electron you come into and out of

this perceived existence, you are entangled in the fabric of the universe and to all beings. Although the electron is seemingly minute on its own, it is the same and as big as the universe in its entirety. Your flicker must be a true one. If you fail you must return and try again and again. If you fail continually, the damage to all around builds up with every generation and your plane of existence will age like a biological cell. By refusing to follow your connections to instinct, you leak energy from this place and make it sick. The evidence of this is all around you and is plain to see. A great deal of damage had been done to the human consciousness even before the Romans.

If you imagine yourself as a radio, you have the ability to tune into all of the available stations. But you choose the tacky commercial station with its brainless harlequin DJs.

Because of your devotion to the economic god, you near a crossroads. You have three options, and the reason that there are three options is because this is the minimum number of points you need to create this perceived universe. The options are as follows:

Do nothing.

Change something.

Change everything.

Timorous, the majority of you choose, as always, the middle path. If this makes sense to you, than carry on, because the forests will regrow and the oceans will replenish regardless. You just won't be around to see it.

9

Let me now take you back to people of long ago, so you may learn by them and mend your ways. I will choose those who lived on the land where I live today. The principles of their living can be applied to many people around the world. They lived lives that were full and happy. They perceived life in ways incomprehensible to you. If you want to understand every facet of human nature and psychology, you need only examine the lives of these people. If only you could. Remember that these words are a struggle and cannot fully transcribe the depth of my feelings. I encourage you to focus and, if you can, try to go back to a time when you were a child playing. Let these words catalyse your consciousness from this golden era of your life. A time when you were indeed at your wisest.

Children chose their parents from before they were born. They are actually older than them. When growing, this precious wisdom needed to be nurtured, because although wiser and older than their parents, they were new here and their parents were not. This child would continue to emerge from the womb throughout life. Encouraged to play like a kitten, exploring, learning to use these alien senses and build his or her new consciousness. Guided by their emotions, and they were also told how they were created by the teachers who knew such things. Gods and deities were used to describe the emotional force and its colours so that it would be better understood and communicated. This training was essential to a happy and uncomplicated life.

We as teachers were not here to control, but to empower. The priority was to protect the child from the problems caused by the misuse of knowledge. This was achieved by a community knitted tightly together, yet fluid and enabling great individual independence. This could again be likened to the hydrogen bond. A child, if raised in the correct way, does not need beating or training like an animal. This child will understand respect and will not bring pain to his family. Of course some children were different, and with wise intuition and counsel, these differences were realised as strengths. The child's education would be tailored to these strengths. The children were guided in such a way that they could find the path they had set upon before the womb. All of their actions and dialogue with the world would have an impact far into the future. The tiniest of things from the touch of a leaf, to how they felt when touching that leaf would have a profound effect on the future.

You see now why the most highly trained became builders. This is also why a simple task, such as sweeping a floor, can feel so rewarding.

As the education of life continued, and their chosen paths found them again, they would enter into adulthood as strong men and women and continue their work. By being alive we are in a state of perpetual prayer. Every thought and action is a form of praying, and all of these prayers are answered. This is why such important guidance was needed from generation to generation and, if entirely broken, the consequences will be alarming.

This is how we are all put to work. Never believe that you are unemployed. All of the time you are alive you are working. Controlling this whirling energy in your mind and focusing it is your work, and you can help crystallise it by your actions. Without the guidance that the children of the past had, you must focus into that emotional communication from us. This emotion, calling you back home to reunite you with your origins, is all you should follow. Your work in life is to simply walk home down your particular track and guide others there along their paths. Just as the Silk Road was never a single defined track, the way home has to follow in the right direction, but is not set in stone. Each way has its barriers and ways to overcome them. This is why we are fascinated by stories of conflict and journeys, and of heroes who resolve that conflict.

When reaching adulthood, it was time to think of the next generation. I want you now to realise that these were a people of great divinity, who lived in a world where the male spirit was one-third and the female two-thirds. Trapped as we are by our bodies and by the cycle of birth and death, the very fibre of our being leaks out of us. This is why we age and die. We are made from an infinite number of quantum pulses that form our physical bodies. Every pulse is conscious and is looking to find its way back to its origins. Throughout our illusion of time, some of these pulses or particles find their way back ahead of us. This could be described as a fight between matter and antimatter, with antimatter gradually gaining the upper hand. So we age and as a result must die.

People used to be able to control this and reverse it, living for centuries. This used to be a matter of choice. You see, your work takes a lot longer than the average current lifetime. So some chose to live longer in their current life in order to carry on this work, or a particular task, more seamlessly. There are some people on this world right now who are doing this, but you would never know who, because they shun fame. It is important that they do this now, for it is getting harder to choose suitable parents these days. Even the most loving of parents often lacks the required wisdom now. This way, of staying on, needs an incredible amount of stamina. You try working an eight-hundred-year shift without a rest.

So to prevent this exhaustion and to keep our work fresh, we die and are reborn until we have achieved our goal. This is why I condemn suicide or a life lived badly or ordinarily. You will just have to come back and do it again and again and again. And on top of that you will have to make amends for your mistakes or wrongdoings before you can again take up the path, and no wrongdoing is greater than the pain you cause to people who love you when you take your life. Be understanding, listen to emotion and always remember you are never alone, even if it seems that way. Even if you are old and nobody seems to listen, there are those who need you and value you. They cannot get home without you. If you think the economic god forces you to do mundane work, then you must change your view of that work and see its value to the future. It will have some, no matter what it is. Or you must liberate yourself and create a new role for yourself. Be daring but be calculating. But we will need to return, so we need lives to live and to create those lives. This involves the harnessing of that most powerful of forces, and it must be harnessed with care, for it is more dangerous now when combined with the other onerous knowledge that was bestowed on mankind.

Like a wild-eyed rearing mass of power, sex must be controlled or it will drag us along uncontrollably and dash us in its wake. This tenet of wisdom has unfortunately become a little misunderstood. Especially by those damned corrupt institutions. You cannot run away from sex's power. You must not punish yourself with guilt or believe that abstinence is the path to divinity. The belligerent belittling of sex belies its beatitude. When we fail to understand sexual desire, what it means and the right way to deal with it, we open the door to the twisted perversions that blight our world, the soulless acts of sex that prevent any real fulfilment.

When people reached sexual maturity in mind and body, they were educated, very thoroughly, by people who were responsible and right for the task. This education taught sex as a sacred and divine prayer. By undertaking this act correctly, the man can touch the creator goddess and the woman will manifest herself as the goddess and touch the conscious power of creation. A man can only reach this divine source of energy through the woman. The act of sex is metaphysical and deep.

Then I must explain that because people thought in many deeper layers than now, they would find lovers for each layer. They would grow by making love to those who would resonate with those different parts of themselves. These were still the basis of deep relationships and were understood on a completely different level. This was not the same as wanton promiscuity.

This act of sex with a few selected partners was deep and fulfilling. There were those who had a talent and a need for others, just as there were those who paired for life, finding this resonance at all depths in one person. The situation was different for everyone, and by correctly tuning into his or her instincts, they avoided any of the problems you may be thinking of, like sexual jealousy or disease. Both of these were virtually nonexistent back then.

Many divine acts of sex and the initiation into sex took place on those sacred circular sites. You must think in opposites to come close to the thought of your ancestors. Your polarity has switched and you run from what you need and feel rather than embracing it. We do not die. What we see as the ending of life is the travelling to a place that cannot be perceived, let alone described, even by those that were here millennia ago. We all leave behind a corpse, but we move to a place outside of time and matter. We either return again or we make it onwards once we have found a way. Do not think that we return just to Earth, or even as a life form, as you think of it. We can move in and out of an infinite number of universes that are created and end constantly. Our journey can be breathtakingly long, yet exist outside time. We can appear as a breeze, a sparkle of light, flicker of flame or even an unheard sound. We can come back as a fleeting feeling of calm in the minds of anyone living, and then be gone again, just as quickly, for another rebirth. Some of us are so holy, good and wise, we leave as a child or even babe in arms.

When we had sex and achieved it in the correct way, we practised our move towards death. For the feeling of death is like the climax of deep ritual sex multiplied by many orders of magnitude. It may be hard for you to think of death as an incredible, pleasurable experience. But this is the truth. We feel as if we are in the throes of passion. We are torn from our earthly existence with a deeply sumptuous mix of agony and ecstasy; we try to scream, but if anything only a gasp is heard by the living. So as we slip into our last moments of this particular life, we experience a stillness of time, clarity of thought and feeling. It is as if our ears open and our hearing is restored to perfection, the tinnitus of worldly distraction vanquished. Time stops for us. We stand on the edge of a great vastness and we may see things as if dreaming, yet we realise that we are waking from a dream.

Because of the timeless void we stand in, we may be here for a long time. It may seem like weeks or even years. And because of the timelessness of this place, these phenomena will occur, even if to the outside we seem to have been taken quickly. We may even have our own little adventure; we will be confused and a child again; we may be able to go back and punch that bully on the nose or make love for the first time again. We will undertake this in a dreamlike way, just accepting the surreality for what it is. But it is our chance to harmonise our mistakes or at least improve on the things we should improve upon. During this time we will come face to face with all of those we have hurt, no matter how little or how much. If you have killed or committed an act of violence on someone, they will be there, and it is up to them how they act and how they choose to deal with you. In life you would have taken your victim's power, now they will judge you and hold all of your power. It will be up to them to decide the rest of your journey and put on to you a share of their burden of errors. This can explain why the warriors of the past cared little about death and had no fear of it. If they had wronged in their lives or were impatient to settle old scores, they would fight with a view to dying in battle. But they would not of course commit suicide. When this phase is over, which to the time of the living was barely a trace of a split second, you will then melt into energy and be absorbed into the embrace of the conscious force.

IO

You may wonder why we feel grief when we lose someone we love. Well, to explain this and many other conundrums, we must understand that we are here making the best of a bad situation. This does not mean that life has to be miserable. It just means that it requires great effort and a life lived as a prayer. Because you have been made as part of a process towards a remaking of the energy that forms you, understand that there has to be give and take. Your societies were bonded together by a powerful love that exists on many levels, depending on our relationship with people. You will also find yourself needing to help strangers in trouble because of this, and it makes you find common ground with people different from you. But the irony is, in order to bond you together, the feeling must be sufficiently strong. You feel physical pain at the loss of someone, because of the strength of this feeling. This is unavoidable, and is the only way of doing things whilst you are here. People you meet throughout your life will become part of you and you part of them, so you lose something personal with each one's parting.

You must reverse your view of the heavens also. The power that holds the Earth together and controls it emanates from a tiny black hole in its centre. The material of the Earth is the residual matter left behind by a filtering process. The whole material universe is constructed by black holes of many sizes. This is the source of gravity for each mass. Our universe behaves the same way as the atomic world. Nature simply repeats itself, layer upon layer. This is why people worshipped the ground and its depths. If we look in, if we could stare to the centre of the world, we would see through to the edge of the universe. The energy that is lost from life is drawn to this place.

You see now how you have been made to perceive the opposite of reality. No wonder you find life so confusing. Some of this energy is channelled at certain places. These are the true divine places and exist on land and beneath the sea. Some have even been buried by our cities, but they are never entirely hidden. And so it happened that a force would come and change with a deadly patience our view of the world and the universe. A force so cunning and powerful that it would override our minds throughout many generations, with changing and more powerful phases to its mission.

Two things happened within a period of a dozen years or so. One event was intended to change human consciousness.

The other event was an attempt to protect us and retrieve the status quo. Each of these events happened over varying timescales and global places, embodying a form that best suited its needs towards its intended people. But we will concern ourselves with the expanding city-state of Rome. Rome's success in its mission is plain to see. The fact that I used the phrase 'status quo' a few sentences ago is evidence enough. Their version of history and their architecture, an amalgam of ideas they stole, are around us and in us constantly. We glory in their military accomplishments and their efficiency of conquest. We glory in their mimics, such as the megalomaniac dwarf Napoleon, who gained providence with the same help as the others of his needy kind. I wonder how long it will be before people see Hitler in this way? After all, he was of the same ilk. But the Romans were not one dictator or just a greedy city-state; they were a way of being and thinking. The greatest confidence trick in the history of humankind was the great achievement of the Romans. To succeed, it had to capture a source of sacred power from where it could launch itself to the world, in any future form it desired. This was achieved by an inadequate runt of a man.

Do you see, the greater the insecurity in a being, the greater their potential for manipulation? Have you ever wondered why dictators are such loathsome people? It is because they loathe themselves and lust for power. They are also the most progressed of thugs. A thug is the end manifestation of the work of the others. They come in all colours and creeds, from the delinquent to the dictator. They exist to cause distress to the innocent. You may do all you can to deal with them and be free of consequence. Thugs have long forgotten the reason they are here and cannot see beyond this time and place. Claudius was the last one expected to achieve what he did. With the help of the others he was bestowed with charisma and cunning. We were the trusted sacred keepers of the truth, but some saw their allegiance with the others, our enemies. Against even their own hearts, they laid the path for Rome.

CAESAR

Alone at night, with thoughts of ambition consuming all the fibres of his body, Caesar dreamed of power. He was fool-hardy with money, seeing it as only a tool to buy influence. This in itself proved that greed was not his primary motivator. Aware of his mortality and driven by the needs of a conqueror, he made himself vulnerable. His vulnerability served the others, as his time and place on Earth made him a worthy, no, priceless tool.

At his lowest ebb, after failing to seduce a teenage girl, he became all too aware of the fickle brevity of his life and the lives of all men. Reaching middle age and with thinning hair, he knew that time was drawing away and mediocrity loomed. And so it was that a bitterness rose in him. A trembling powerful rage consumed him and squeezed him until all that was left was a vulnerable babe of a man. Nakedness and fear pierced his skin as his ego fell. This mask, this shield that all people use to shelter themselves from the bitter storm of nature, was all the more important to a man like Caesar. When you choose to walk amongst the hardest and cruellest winds, this ego-mask protects you from the coldest and quickest of deaths.

And so, at this low trembling ebb, on his knees naked on a marble floor on a Roman summer evening, he was offered some comfort by a visitor.

'Why so sad?'

Caesar jumped up, the tears cooling on his face.

'Who . . . where are you? How did you get in here?'

Out of the shadows stepped a figure in a cloak. Disarmingly demur, and lifting back the hood of the cloak, stood a young woman, of course beautiful in a sexually charged and powerful way. With her soft, seductive voice, she calmed his fear, but only a little, as the puzzle of her presence and the oddity of her intrusion reignited and challenged Caesar's intellect. But she did not engender enough fear for him to cry out for protection, nor did she initiate any feelings of lust. Her seduction was in the rightness she made him feel in her presence. He knew that for some reason she should be there.

'I am here to help you. To save you. To make you fulfil your destiny. To grace your every move. To guide all of your actions. To destroy your enemies, including that of doubt, and to carry you through to the greatest levels of what it is to be a man, a conqueror, a God. And no man, no whim of the heavens or will of human shall stop you. Every decision you make will be flawless, every horse you ride will carry you onwards with no trip or throw, and all will love and fear you, ally and enemy, from shore to shore of this world and the next. I promise you victory, immortality and fame. You will be a beacon for millennia and even the Sun will move as you wish. Do you accept this or reject me?'

Caesar grabbed for his robe and covered his nakedness. He was not ashamed of this, but it represented the armour of his ego and filled him with the illusion of courage, as did lifting his nose to the air with a subtle squint of his eyes. Composure regained now in this strange situation with its curious comfort and truthfulness.

'Who are you, what power do you think you possess that could do this for me?' Intrigue and hope for such help was tempting him, regardless of the improbability of such fortune.

'Do you accept this or reject me?'

'I don't know what you are, who you are, to get past the guards. Is this a joke? I have little time or care for jokes.'

'Tomorrow, your fortunes will change. You will benefit from friendships you have, your influence will grow from these friendships and a calm will fill your soul; your friends will lift you high then fall away, but only with my influence. I give you this as three months' grace, not long enough by any means to fulfil your destiny, but long enough to show you the change. Do not be fooled by their subtlety but be awed by their brevity if you should deny me. Do not forget this meeting because in three months I will ask you again: Do you accept this or reject me?'

And with that she pulled up her hood and walked past the flickering torch and into the shadows. Vanishing.

We do not know how Caesar spent that night, how he digested this event, but sure enough his fortunes prospered and his way was cleared, a light was lit that showed him the way and a guiding hand pushed him away from any wrong-footed ways. He truly began to win at life and all his ambitions began to be fulfilled.

And his friendship held him high, his bounty knew no bounds as unofficially he rose in power, or at least began to rise because one quarter of a year (as we know now) is far too brief to be a conqueror, even with all the help in the world.

A reminder beckoned. Walking through the streets and knowing so confidently now that no assassin was looking out for him, Caesar took the bows and greetings of the loving people and ate an apple gifted to him by a trader. Then, amongst the anonymous shadows of plebs, a face struck him and drew his eyes to make contact with theirs. This was a tall man with shortish grey hair and a longish grey beard. Wearing a sleeveless leather smock and with the gait and limbs of a blacksmith or swordsmith. His eyes twinkled with charisma and that feeling of right and truth.

His glittering smile and white straight teeth beckoned over Caesar, who, with the hope of another gift from a loyal admirer, walked towards him.

'Can I interest you in a gift?'

'You may,' Caesar replied with aristocratic reward.

The man handed Caesar a box. Caesar tried to open it but the catch wouldn't budge.

'This is broken,' Caesar stated, his eyes looking down the bridge of his nose towards his inferior.

'That depends if you accept or reject.'

Caesar opened his eyes guardedly. He knew the asker of this question and he knew he had to reply, but ego and intellect were all the more in control now and so he handed back the plain box and walked away. The man neither called him back nor called out in insult and Caesar went on his way.

In the morning he woke with all the hope and confidence he had grown used to. The rivers of life and luck continued to flow as he pleased, but little by little the tide was turning and a tiny taste of tragedy would ebb towards him.

Rising, he was bemused by the lack of obedient slaves and a faint smell he recognised – was it from the victory or defeat of battle? An eerie silence distended throughout the villa. So he wandered through the opulence, the torches still lit, even though dawn must have broken more than an hour ago. He called out,

'Water! Bring me my water!'

No reply as his words echoed off the sumptuous stone and through the cavernous rooms and cloisters. He edged onwards with tested courage through the villa, past the frescoes and the plants and then into the courtyard. The colours of the sky and stone, vibrant in the Sun's intensity, hiding the coming ferocity. As Caesar's walk and time unfurled, he crossed the courtyard to the servants' quarters and then through the door.

Hardly could he bring his senses to the fore as he looked up at the beams and saw all his household hanging by their feet with their arms stretched towards the floor. In a forced prayer to the underworld that had taken them. Not a drop of blood or mark of passion on their faces. It seemed they had been taken with a supernatural and hidden speed, no wounds or mercy.

Caesar ran through the room, the slaughtereds' hands cuffing him in an absurd rebuke. He sweated and feared and held up his robe to stop him tripping. Up to the side door. He burst it open to be confronted by an empty street: no bird, no dog, no people. No time or vein of life was present, the stillness primeval and wickedly overbearing. He ran down the street calling, but to no avail.

The emptiness, so foreboding. Abandoned carts and objects, dropped as if the owners were whipped away by a twirling wind. And then, in all this stillness, a glimpse of movement between the streets, fleeting in the distance. Caesar ran and shouted:

'Wait!'

To no avail. No turning back, he ran to the junction looking left and right. Again the shape just disappeared into a doorway on the left.

Caesar ran, obedient to the temptation, through the gnarled plebe door and into a windowless room. The darkness amplified by the brightness outside, his eyes unable to adjust.

'Where are you?'

'Who are you?'

Silence and obscurity prevailed and only the insanity of the situation remained. The sweat ran down Caesar's unwashed face, his short breaths punching into the darkness.

'Show yourself.'

Shocked by a wisp of light appearing through a high-up slit in the wall, he spun round to leave, only to find that the door had silently closed behind him. Those shallow breaths fluttered all the faster and the sweat flowed down his face. A feeling of company great and small emanated from the air, filling the room, exhuming the remaining courage from Caesar and dashing it against the walls. The presence rose as if to rumble in his soul and at the crescendo it spoke,

'All are gone, so what is power if no man is to witness it?'

Caesar was silent in awe.

'You are all that's left. I have killed all in Rome and have the power to move further still. Do you see what I can do?

'Mine is the control of everything and I had the good grace to choose you. You had the audacity to throw my gift back in my face. I can create more woe than you can bear, I can bring you back so that all you see are the victories of your enemies at your expense. I can send the hordes of Hades and I can slowly make you burn!'

A supernatural grip clamped on Caesar's throat and raised him in the air. The light from the window shone into his face and blinded him, the fear so great he was paralysed, except for the negating of his bladder. He whimpered, sweated and urinated. In his fear and with all the capacity he could muster, through his constricted throat he gasped,

'I accept.'

I I

The allegiance of the others undid so much. It succeeded by taking away the people's faith in us. They did not listen any more. Petty squabbles turned into wars and hatred. As the antidote to the burdensome knowledge of technology, we had to be rendered impotent. The others had gone too far and unchecked with their twisting of reality, and because they had reached greater strength than us, we failed. The king of the land where I now live allowed his family to become Romanised. Others followed throughout the land, changing their buildings and clothes, even their own tongues they twisted. Like sheep following the shepherd to the abattoir, they followed the fashion of Rome. Over several generations, the descendants of these kings allowed the legions of Claudius to embark unopposed in the land I had watched repel Caesar all of those years ago.

We were ignored and set aside, whilst council was taken up

with my opposing kind. From the height of my being I trembled and felt as a man, weak and fearful. You know these stories are true. They are always retold, differing in their content, but of the same essence. They bubble up from your subconscious, reminding you, warning you. So, after seventeen years of Roman conquest, the rest of our holy kind scattered to other nearby islands where we could carry on our resistance longer. Our few remaining followers came with us and we sought to find the depths of our powers and dive into the dimension of truth to change what had happened or set a path to re-right the world. We set ourselves up to be taken where we could wait with patience. This would involve setting up a trick and allowing ourselves to die.

We let it be known that there was a sacred place of learning, where all our knowledge was kept. We knew they would believe this, for to them everything had to have a physical place. We led the Romans to an island off the far west coast.

Darkness fell and we waited amongst the rustle of the trees in the moonlit summer evening. Aware of the manoeuvres across the water, the preparation of troops. Legio quarta decima Gemina numbered more than five thousand men, formed originally by Caesar and here by no irony. Around two thousand veterans from another legion, a vexillation of Legio vigesima, joined them. Their skills made better because their ranks were swelled by a thousand traitors. Our own people.

The flames of a thousand torches flickered amongst a

luminous sea of Roman armour mirrored in the straits. The smell of burning tallow tainted the air on our side. The rumbling of thousands of alien tongues, the clanking and banging of engineering works and the preparation of war machines. The impatient whinnying of countless horses, the odd eruption of laughter and the occasional felling of a tree. We waited, preparing our ruse, ready to play into the hands of those partially sensing fools.

The dawn lifted and the full energy of the season grew. The birds sang. The Romans' confidence was all part of our manipulation. The landscape on our side undulated, a strip of fertile fields to the west of which stood deep, ancient forests. This gave us space we did not need but the Romans craved, as they huddled together at the thickly wooded far bank. The powerful tidal sea river divided us for now.

We stood with ranks of many warriors, fearless of death, because there is no death. Powerful women as numerous as the stars and of angelic beauty moved in front of the warriors and began to wail. As they did, the ground of the far bank quaked and a mighty blast of wind blew against the Romans' shields, pushing them down on to their knees. The women lifted their hands and faces towards the Sun, the pitch of their cries changed and the Sun magnified to blinding intensity. Their cries carried on the white light as the legions dropped their shields and covered their eyes. The noise faded to silence, the light vanished into twirling sparks and the wind became a breeze. The Romans fumbled in transient blindness and deafness.

I loved to watch as we built their confidence and then crushed it. This, you see, would always make them doubt the truth of what they saw that day, would spread myth to the whole world, and when it reached the ears of those who understood in a far-off time, our story and therefore we would again be real.

I saw in the mind of their commander, Gaius Suetonius Paulinus, a lustful drive for fame and *auctoritas*. The Romans were in the pangs of terror. A fear most had not experienced since children, when overhearing late-night stories of demons and death. Their senses returning, looking to each other for comfort they couldn't find. Frightened faces, young and old, the myth of manhood lost to primitive terror. Their red tunics beneath their chainmail armour soaked with fear, their shining helms causing an intensity of sweat to burn their eyes, their emblem of Capricorn no more than childish art. I moved unseen amongst their ranks and saw, cowering from me, the others, my enemy.

I looked a steady gaze at them. I astounded them by raising my hands and banishing all fear in the Roman ranks. I swept it aside and ushered back their courage. I filled them with a drunken glee and whispered to their commander to shout 'Advance!'

They filled their boats, swam with their horses, crossed

by any means, full of the lust for blood and for victory. The treacherous eddies claimed a few, now lost under more than a million tides. Their machines fired burning barrels of tallow across the straits and fired a hail of spears, flaming arrows followed, through the air with a wisp and thudding into the earth. Crashes and explosions of burning caskets of fat splashed fire on the ground. We beat our shields and goaded, abused and drew them forth. We retreated to the depths of the woods, leading a path through fields for them to follow.

They followed, but only up to a point, again filled with a distrust and fear of fighting at a disadvantage; they halted after three miles and faced the woods as if the trees were a massed rank of enemy. An army trained to fight on open plains had little strategy for an enemy amongst the trees. That night they built a quadrangle camp, the ramparts with rounded corners and four large gates, seated within a steep bank and ditch.

The morning broke to an eerie silence, punctuated only by birdsong, stillness but for the rustle of trees and the night mists dissolving. The morning call sounded in the Roman camp and the muster began; tentatively some of the troops checked the watchtowers, fearing a sight that might plant demons in their minds, but the guards were fine, no horrific mutilation or lakes of blood. A steady gaze over the forest was met with nothing, not even the stirring of a bear, the remaining mist clinging to the trees.

Later that morning, Paulinus sent out three bands of scouts to probe a way into the woods, one hundred and twenty men on horse making each party. He would not be drawn to fight in the forest. It was not the Roman way to form ranks amongst the trees. But the men were becoming restless. Their fear could turn on their commander, and although attached to the might of Rome, they were all alone a long way from home, huddled for safety amongst a deadly beauty.

One of the bands of scouts returned, with a hostage found foraging at the forest fringe, a bitter, resentful man, who had studied our ways his entire life, but had no aptitude, no soul for our work. His bitterness whispered to him the need for revenge, to vanquish those who had removed his purpose. We called him Syrth.

Syrth as a child was different, born with a darkness that other children derided. His parents feared and rejected him, his early life was lonely and he sought belonging in the Druids. We felt his pain, and some of us tried to take him into our fold. But he was full of acrimony. He banished his tribe from his life and lived apart from men. I knew one day we could harness his malevolence.

So, amongst comfort and wine, he told of a way through the woods where the forest path was unguarded and came up to open ground, a subtle hill with a grove of trees atop. He spoke of such places on the island, of their importance to us, but he, this betrayer, knew nothing of what they meant.

He drew maps and worked for twenty days; he told the Romans where to find forage safely and where to take crops. He told them that the whole island had grown fearful of this great Roman warlord and had hidden away in the forest. He said they would meet no resistance.

Paulinus confirmed these stories by sending out scouts; they found abandoned villages with warm hearths, livestock left untended. Of course all of the food was taken and the homes burnt. Through this traitor they found the cracks and paths, the way to sink the Eagle's claw into the flesh of the land. They soon had mastery of the material surface, and with their confidence raised up high they mustered to advance.

They did not know the traitor was sent by us. As punishment for a life passed, we had denied him the knowledge he so surely craved in this one, so his darkness and anger would lead him to this. You see, some believe that they can master fate, make history, turn the tide or make or break a people, but this is not so. Some things must come to pass and seem a great injustice. But there is a need for things to be a certain way, because all events seek to form a balanced future. Only we can see through time and understand the importance of all events, even the tiniest that lie in the infinite roots of creation.

As the dawn began to break and the first bird sang, the western doors flung open on the camp. Hanging in pairs, each door was four times the height of a man and half as wide as it was high. Made from flat wide planks of oak, they bore the scars of a long northward journey, a testament to a campaign of trespass. The ramparts filled with archers as three large bundles of hazel were rolled into the V-shaped ditch in front of the gate. A timber bridge slid over the bundles and two centuries of eighty men each spilled out. Swords drawn, shields forward, turning left and right to cover the gate as the rest of the legion followed.

The main detachment of five thousand left, stamping in unison on the bridge, marching west as a column, their pristine armour soon fouling in their dust cloud. They found their way through the woods, led by our treacherous friend. The Romans, younger and veteran alike, moved fearfully through the woods. Memories of ambush, men disappearing from the rear, only to be found up ahead with their lungs made into wings and hanging by their entrails. Some remembered the sight, some the smell. For some the screams for 'mother' would ring in their ears, daily, as if shouted again for real. But this didn't happen, not this time. They had made good sacrifices to Mars, and Fortune was his consort. Like Caesar, over a hundred years before, Paulinus was supremely confident and knew in his heart that he couldn't fail. All around, our invisible presence prevailed.

The path opened, as they had been told. A gentle hill towards a grove, half a mile away. Uncommonly large and beautiful oaks, unassuming, unpretentious, no ditch or fort or rampart. Paulinus cried 'Halt' and summoned the traitor, sternly warning him of the consequences of trickery. The traitor explained that we believed that fate alone would protect this place, that nature was its guardian. Calmness fell upon the area, still and relaxing, the Sun breaking through a cloud, illuminating and warming. The commander, on horseback at the front of his men, stared from the dark crack of the forest across the emerald grass to the distant grove. The men behind betrayed their nerves by their clattering fidgets, so to keep cohesion he waved on the advance and out they poured, on to the field, facing the grove. They formed up from their long marching column and into their ranks to prepare for battle, steadying their minds and checking their weapons and armour, centurions giving rousing speeches to their cohorts and stern warnings about cowardice. The triplex acies formed, flanked by cavalry, as twenty scouts moved ahead to spy us, their enemy.

The scouts moved with caution around the grove, leaning forward, their chests on their horses' backs to see amongst the trees. Seeing nothing but cold, silent darkness, and with every instinct telling them otherwise, they drew their swords and began to trot amongst the oaks, ducking the branches and hardly breathing.

Meanwhile, Paulinus modified the formation of his men, drawing them forward and surrounding the grove, from their straight formation all facing forward, to three units facing the grove as spokes on a wheel. This challenged his ideas about formation and concerned him regarding communication to his men, so he sent six men far out to signal with flags, in sight of each other, Paulinus and the commander of each of the three 'spokes'. So confident was he about the words of his pet traitor, he made this formation without the report from his scouts.

The Romans stood silent, their training and discipline and hearts ridged, still, with pride and courage, the uncommonly warm midday August Sun heating their armour, increasing their thirst for water and blood. Some wondered why they were facing trees and not men, others were blank, their individuality absorbed by the Roman machine. But none spoke or wavered, not one slouched or bowed his head. Not one out of five thousand.

Being in the open gave them confidence. This is how they

were trained; this is how wars are fought, battles won and 'right' extended across the darker Earth. This is the way it would always be, such was supernatural favour bestowed on Rome. So they didn't flinch when a horse whinnied and galloped out from amongst the trees of the grove. The horse, whitish roan and unburdened by tack or rider, trotted to Paulinus. Stopping short of the commander, it stood still as if it had an invisible rider. The officers looked at each other with a wry grin, to hide their discomfort. Paulinus was bemused; he had learnt that the Britons were illiterate, yet carved deep on the horse's back was a bloody '*NULLUS*'.

This act of defiance, although acts of defiance are always expected, was troublesome, and held within it the danger of affecting morale. You see, the Romans knew that to win wars all you needed to do was to have supreme morale. You do this by building a myth of gods and patriotism, you amplify it by propaganda through sheer numbers of men, and you sustain it by winning. You do this, you win, by manipulating the morale of the enemy by inducing panic. You can always induce panic in the enemy, regardless of his numbers. All you need is to be a better choreographer than him. All the best generals knew this; they knew that stories of the numbers of enemies killed were false; most would run from you; the sheer mechanics of slaughtering thousands of the enemy was impossible. Pan is the god of war, not Mars.

Those Paulinus now faced could not be allowed to run, for

to him they were the morale of his enemy. This morale, if allowed to escape and re-form, would stop the conquest of Britain. This was the Britons' truth and reason for being. It was an antithesis to Rome that could not be bought or seduced.

Paulinus had the lie of the land; he held in his head a map of the island and had formed a strategy of conquest. He knew that we would gather on our sacred places and he had to destroy them and us.

Paulinus wondered if he should have brought barrels of tallow to ignite the grove. Could he summon them up from the main camp? This, though, he surmised would take too long, being over six miles away. This would necessitate the construction of another camp, as the day would ebb away, costing momentum. He sought the glory of facing the enemy in the forest, of fighting eye to eye and bringing with it indomitable morale to finish the campaign swiftly.

The command was sounded and instantly communicated by the signallers. The three units advanced into the grove, the fearful affected more by the whispers from the forest, the darkness playing on their nerves, their eyes darting side to side. The front ranks, using their shields, parted the thicket of hawthorn ringing the edge of the grove. The following ranks trampled it, breaking through to the relatively open woodland floor, canopied by giant, ancient oaks that stretched far above.

Some noticed that after a while the grove became larger

than the few acres it seemed from the outside, and before long they were trapped in a seemingly dense and dark forest of immeasurable size. The pathway behind them showed no sign of the edge of the grove. The Romans became afraid, but Paulinus shouted, 'Trickery.' He told them that they would either defeat the enemy or die with their commander and standard. They advanced still further, the shade as complete as if it was a moonlit night.

Then, through the deep dark oaks, came the distant thunder of drums. Further still, and the chanting of women and men rose from the depths within the drumming rhythm.

Men and horses stepped cautiously onward towards the sounds. Swords drawn, they were wide-eyed, hearing every footfall and snapping twig. The cold shaded air causing a chill on recently sweating bodies, alert to every breeze and breath. Silence amongst the ranks. Not a sound was spoken, as if an utterance brought certain death. The drums grew louder, the chanting more foreboding, the tension rising with ears pricking and eyes widening. Each of the three units of men had long expected to meet, but all three were still in isolation.

In an instant, shafts of light broke through the trees ahead, as if day had started to break and the edge of the forest was nearing. The light was intensifying, as were the drumming and chanting. Each of the three units saw this before them, regardless of the direction they faced. Drawing nearer, the light lessened the Romans' fear; even the bravest are afraid of total darkness.

The trees gave way to a clearing, and the first of the Romans to cross the edge of the trees were overcome by a feeling of sexual intensity, robbing them of their breath, paralysing every nerve and bringing them to their knees. A crescendo of chanting and pounding rhythmic beats seemed to hammer them down. All around, whirling female spirits screamed with fervent rage. The remaining troops ran forward from the forest to be brought down, covering their ears and clenching their eyes, unable to protect their senses.

In an instant all sound stopped, the light dimmed to that of a normal summer's day, and tentatively the Romans gathered themselves and rose. A gentle meadow, with butterflies and bees dancing from flower to flower, of heavenly peace and beauty. Stretching far ahead, the meadow gently rose to form a horizon in the distance. The cold sweat of fear turned to the sweat of the Sun's heat on hot armour. All of the legion emerged and mustered to their commander. They gathered their senses and ploughed on through the meadow to find us.

Paulinus asked the traitor where the drumming and chanting had come from, but the traitor was unable to answer. The limits of his knowledge had been reached. The legion marched forward, tramping flat the meadow grass, as if to engage a close enemy. Eyes fixed forward, obeying the will of Paulinus.

As the legion sailed through the vast waves of meadow grass, the ground began to quake, bringing them down, clattering and stumbling like drunks and shrieking in fear. Horses bucked and threw their riders; some of the men pinned themselves down in the long grass like children huddling under a blanket. Paulinus remained steady and unwavering, strangely unafraid.

A fissure appeared ahead of them and out poured an icy volcanic blast. The power of the blast flattened the grass all around, revealing the cowering legion. Mist and smoke surrounded them thickly, cutting each man off from the other, alone, including Paulinus.

A voice whispered to him.

'If you fulfil your mission, you will lose.'

But he knew his gods and name were with him, he knew that he would not stop, the glory immediately before him was all he craved. The ash, like mist, brought visions of far-reaching terror to him and all his men, death and human pain immeasurable amongst uncountable people. But we knew all this was in vain, as we knew that the threshold had been crossed.

The grey flickering mist thinned to the normal day, but the fissure in the ground remained. The agonised lament of future mothers screamed throughout every direction and out of the ground. We climbed calmly from the fissure, looking no more priestlike than any other native adorned by their fashions and tastes. The Romans picked themselves up under the barking orders of Paulinus and his officers; they stood and shuffled back into their ranks, gathering dropped helmets and weapons. We stood fast. No terms were needed to negotiate.

The triplex acies stood ahead, its ranks silent, with armour still mostly polished to a shine, unmoving. The horsemen again upright at the flanks, to chase down any runners, and leave the field with their enemy survivor-less.

We walked calmly towards them. Across the flat meadow grass, a solemn calm, no chants or cries to gods, no fury, no chance of turning back or undoing what had been done. They stood twitching and staring as horses on a start line before a race. We neared and their agony to let loose increased, the air electrified with their desperation.

We walked towards them, right up to them, we stood and faced them right up to their shields and stared into their eyes, one by one. We had no weapons that they could see, no spears or shields, just calm and courage, and we matched their iron will.

Paulinus raised his hand, staring – steely – up ahead. His officers looked around to transmit the command; they raised their hands, and so did we.

The hands of the Romans fell, but ours stayed aloft. We looked up at the sky and back again into their eyes; as the swords sliced into our flesh we laughed as if bathing in a waterfall. As the life left our bodies, some of the Romans caught a glimpse of giant shadow men leaping from us into the sky.

The Romans roared and clattered, their leader allowing them the rare chance to break discipline. He had always read of the large enemy fatalities, and laughed at the ignorant, crowd-pleasing scribes. Now for the first time he would learn just how long it would take to butcher a thousand men. Just six hours.

They marched back through the grove, the churned meadow grass soaked with blood, sinking into the ground, uniting with the elements that first made it. The grove this time just a normal piece of woodland. And, as they marched, the magic faded, the memories changed, the fighting no more than normal blood and sweat, flesh as you or me.

No more did they remember the dazzling of the Sun, the strange enormity of the grove, the chanting, the drumming, the earthquakes. But some would have dreams of giant, shadow-like men flying towards the sky.

There are no sacred groves; no special objects or places, for these are just material things, made of this world and by men. There is no magic power – as if it could be so. But there is a subtle truth, ungraspable by man, that sits in every corner of a vast and now unconscious land. It cannot be reached by ritual, or conjecture, or even by chance, but it lives deep within you, no matter who you are.

Leon Jenner

12

We could now carry out our work at a deeper level. We retreated to the core of the Earth and beyond, to the axis.

Our work can be achieved by stillness and the power of thought. We can achieve a great deal by this alone. Creation and creativity has many forms. And by reaching this indescribable depth that we have been operating from, the results reach further. From the axis we were out of reach of our enemies and could take back our power.

But there was one who was sent to prevent Rome from seizing the last of the sacred places where the last of the free could be caught. He died about a dozen years before the invasion of Britain. His is a story familiar to you. This story was later hijacked by Rome when they saw its beauty and power. They used his name to forge a second invasion of Europe, and by the institutions they created they committed the greatest blasphemy. He was the earthly focus of the highest philosophy. His story, if truly understood, will quiver your heart and set you free. His divinity channelled into this place and blessed it. The intention was to set straight the path and return it to its true course towards home. He was sent to highlight our common bonds and language and show there are no differences. If you forget what you have been taught about him, the way to the truth is through him. The symbols of his life are our symbols. He is the embodiment of the wisdom that is the master of Druids.

In this way they used the name of our own master to vanquish us who remained. And he embodies the male in his highest form. Through listening to him, the one-third power of man becomes half. I suggest you find him and in a way that requires nothing but the emptiness of your mind and the stillness of your heart between each pulse. He does not relate to just us in this culture. He exists in all cultures and seems different to everyone. Remember, though, no man, no matter how divine, can exist without a woman.

Because of the success of the Romans, darkness deepened at a quickening rate over man. The source of this blackness was impatience. The traitors that were amongst us thought that they could speed up the way home. Man and woman are too idle and happy, they thought. By revealing themselves in dreams, they sowed the seeds of change. Start to control resources, then you may be freer to multiply, they said. More people means more power and more to control. Achieve this by changing plants and animals to suit your needs. This knowledge came as fleeting thoughts. Dreams do not have to be long, nor do they have to come during sleep. All you have to do is influence emotion to spark changes in any life form. Those of us who were sent here to guide you had to begin to fight our own kind who sought to control you in this way. And one of our greatest weapons was the brick. We embodied the technology they taught you in the brick and used it to try to set you back on the correct path.

So people were drawn to wonder and experiment. The results of this are that some must toil whilst others profit. Those who profit resent those who profit more, and the festering prelude to war is established. As numbers multiply, resources are needed more and more. They are finite and must be taken from others in order to survive. And so it goes on. To begin with you were set great challenges. You are here by error and you are slowly finding your way home. You all need each other to achieve this. You must all learn the same divine lessons in order to find your way home. By helping others to lead a good and full life, you help yourself, and you must do this. Unless we all achieve our divinity, we will all be trapped in an endless cycle of birth and rebirth. I know this sounds like a sermon. But it is the truth. I am telling you all of this stuff, and it is laborious and hard for me.

It pains me to have to write it and tell it to you. I know you think it's all fiction or just the excuse to escape from reality a while, but believe me, listen to me and understand the words of these pages. I am here now because I am needed. I have been awoken in a place where I neither belong nor want to be. I had to be reborn after over three decades of suffering and I need respite. Some of us – because I am not the only one who has the damned task of being here – have returned to the places where we were once laid in memory to find our sacred places churned by a plough, or plundered, or smothered over by a river of black tarmac, noise and pollution. Even worse, crushed under an architectural edifice, the product of a damnable institution that thinks they know buildings. An institution most members of which cannot even put up a shelf, yet they call themselves master builders! The same is true of the church. Priests, vicars, or whatever they are called, sitting idle on blocks of stone, smothering our sites and drowning our past. They know only what their higher-up administrators tell them.

My anger rises daily and my patience wears thin with you people. Yes, children are sacred, but for all our sakes, guide them. They are older than you in spirit, but not on Earth. They look to you for structure and guidance. Life is structure and guidance and discipline. Use it, or carry on down the path where unruly thugs are tolerated. The thug is the endpoint, the terminus of the most wrong of roads. Those who want to hurt you by taunt or violence or damage to the things you need and cherish. Do not see the thug as human. They have strayed too far and can only be dealt with when out of this world. Do not think you can reason with them. Pre-emption is the best defence, and from this high order, I can tell you that you can bash 'em. Do this without conversation. Just hit and hit and hit. Believe me, it feels good, and I have told you before, there will be no recompense for your actions. Except from those in this world who serve them. Sometimes, in my more human, darker moments, I take myself to the bad, soul-less areas of towns. Here I disguise myself as a vagrant or elderly stooped vulnerability. I walk or wait and put myself in what seems danger. Sometimes I am surprised by the helpful-ness and guidance of the people, and this gives me hope. But other times some attempt to harm me. They try this because they have become thugs and are now inhuman. Because of their inhumanity, I am free to do with them as I wish. These people would not have existed in the far past. If they had their existence would have been bought to an abrupt end. Why do you tolerate, and even propagate, them now? Don't you see that political correctness paves the way for the next Hitler?

I enjoy the fear on their faces as I end them without the need to lay a finger on them or utter a word. Sometimes I merely set the path for their death and walk away knowing their agonis-ing, prolonged fate. Sometimes I choose to blind or maim them. It depends on my mood. You have got to such a state of affairs that I tire of being pious and holy and now I am feeling human again. I am filled with anger and rage, lusting to expel my fury. For thousands of years I have struggled with patience and calm and piety, but now the time has come where you must be disciplined for making the wrong choices. You have created my twin voice of furious, impious, thundering anger; and from this fury I will wreak vengeance on those who have followed the others and those who are the others.

By now you realise that I have many names, or at least we do. We encompass all octaves of emotion and we sing to you daily. There is no such thing as good or evil, and don't you dare start to say I am the devil. Sometimes I can be. He is no one person or way, but our freedom has brought us problems as your freedom has to you. We are going to get back and the incompetent apprentices that have created this mess will pay.

I am old enough now to be firmly in charge of this place, and you have made it necessary for me to amend things. I say to all the politicians out there, you will know me soon enough. You are holding me and my kind back. Your actions and the benign impotence of the masses that follow you are making me impatient. I have been disturbed from great and important work to be here, because of you. And because of you I keep being disturbed.

Now that I have reached such an age and such power, I will use it. If you want proof of our return, just look at the behaviour of animals, notably the fox. Have you noticed they are getting bolder? Do you see that, slowly, they are beginning to tire of being afraid of you? Like children in a zoo, they are observing an endangered species. I don't need to tell you of the environmental changes, temperature and tectonic shifts, blasts of invisible energy calling destruction. Bear in mind my earlier words of love and wisdom. They are indeed true – but restrained in their meaning by their nature and by yours. You can complain as much as you like about how well written these words are. I am no great writer, I am a venter of rage and ignored provider of attempted wise words. At least the unanswerable monologue stops you from arguing back. I am so sick of explaining myself and proving myself, restraining and retraining to suit you. All I want to do is build. All I want to do is create. This world brought me so much joy, because I could finally do this. But when I needed money in my more earthly life, you, the customer or client, depending on how much you were paying, you stifled it. Time-scales, budgets, yes sir no sir, weak tea, no tea, can't pay you this week, aaaargh! So now I cannot build because I poison the buildings, maimed by the economic god. Can you imagine what this has done to me? To be torn apart by the need to create, yet know that what I create will damage so much – as my polluted mind poisons the details of all I make? Now I resort to hiding in the gauged bricklayer's shed making bits of buildings, remembering and wanting the past, dreaming of what once was and distracting me from my stifled soul.

Forgive my rants, but understand them. I have been called because you are at a crossroads. Some of you have strayed so far. There are those of you who are truly good, and deserving of better, and it is for them that I come. A great generation of you endured great pain with your war caused by the enforced neglect of empire, and all sides suffered. Without the universal soldier, war is impossible, but the universal soldier has proved he is capable of great human things. In the face of such terrible odds and with the just cause of destroying the Nazis, and other states of thuggery, the embodiment of the Victoria Cross-holders and their worldly equivalents is one that is high and holy. The modesty of those that hold this cross lifts them higher. Their sacrifices stemmed from the bond they had with comrade and friend; they performed impassioned, sacred sacrifice. It is this generation that I come for. It is you who have called me, and it is for you that I will make amends. I understand your suffering, your loneliness and your bewilderment with the world. As you fade, I will hold your torch.

I also come for all of those who have been wronged or who have suffered injustice. My guise this time is that of an avenging angel. I see all the wrong in the world and feel your pain, as I did as a fourteen-year-old boy in my bed. The difference now is in my power and will to deal with what is wrong. This applies to all. Whatever causes you pain is your challenge to right. If you are made to suffer, you will be reborn stronger, maybe in the way I was. Set free your passion, unleash your will, but ensure its justification.

In the past and the panic to speed up your progress, greater errors were made to stem the speed of your trials. This ended with us having to wipe you out, except for a few deemed good enough to continue. As I have said before, entire civilisations and peoples – far different from anyone today – once lived here. Time and again they grew, time and again they failed and were reduced. All of this because of the unleashing of knowledge before the time was right. Because we cannot eradicate this knowledge without ending all of you, we struggle.

I am warning you now that we are beginning to consider the possibility of starting again with another species or another world. You were chosen as the path home and you are squandering this privilege like spoilt children. The further away you go, the more you lessen your worth, your viability. We have woken again, but this is for the last time. I have told you the reasons for your failings. I have told you how to change. By allowing your politicians and other leaders to carry on things that you know are wrong, you are bound by a collective guilt. Change it now, change everything, and follow the passionate path. Find those colours and those emotions. See and feel their brilliance. Do not do anything other than that which feels entirely right. You have power, more than you can imagine. You can step into the wonder and depth of life, or you can listen to the 'experts' and follow in their shallow ways. If you tune in, you will know. This is obvious and maybe patronising, but it looks as if it needs to be repeated again and again.

I have had friends who have ended their lives, because they have been made so lost. I knew one who leapt to his death from a cliff on a cold drizzling evening around the time of Easter. I often think of him crying, empty, cold and frightened. Standing perched precariously on the same cliff where those silken giants once stood. Despite his family who loved him, despite his talents and the children he would have one day fathered, he stepped forward. His death reached further than he could have possibly imagined.

At the time I heard of his death, I was looking at a house in need of repair. The house was owned by an old lady who had lived there alone. She had recently died, and at the moment of her death the gutters fell from their brackets and tiles slid from the roof. Her house, her soul and seat of life, reflected the crystallisation of her reality and that crystal lost its integrity as she left. This is what occurs to the world around you if you choose to leave before your time.

And, as you know, you will have to make amends and start all over again. This damage can be reversed by our actions and by having the courage to defy what we have been taught. It is my job to ensure that the fabric of buildings is of the highest integrity. Throughout the past and now I inspect the sites of my projects to see if my workers have driven in every nail correctly, laid every brick with truth or poured concrete with the correct mindset. I also inspect other buildings that are old and were built at a time when all of us builders knew the true art of building. Sometimes I see that, despite their age and the passion of the men who built them, subsequent changes have altered the happiness of the structure. You will know this if you live in such a house. It will speak to you and tell you what is wrong. It may whisper or shout, depending on the damage.

I see some buildings that have become so wounded they beg for death. Some houses from the time of Victoria, although well built, have problems with their materials. The materials, like the bricks, for example, were made in a place where children were exploited and the poor put upon. The energy of their unhappiness was absorbed into each brick and therefore into your home or place of work. This can be counteracted by placing a structure or sculpture in your home, a sculpture of gauged bricks made and laid the correct way. Even just one brick made with care and placed in a wall or even loose under the floor will suffice. This will take away the sorrow from the fabric of your walls and create balance. It is virtually impossible now for me to tell customers about these very real problems. They wouldn't understand any more, or they would think I'm mad. This is why changing the entirety of your minds takes such courage. You are the bricks that define human existence, and a structure is as perfect as its most flawed and worst-laid brick.

Care should be taken especially with the fine-cut bricks above the doors and windows of older houses. This is the work of the gauged bricklayer and is the very highest art. These are the jewels of the structure, the embellishment of a deep pride long forgotten by most. They should be repaired by someone with the deeper skills and wisdom, or your home or any other building will suffer. Take care in your choice of builder. Many factors go into such work, and these go far beyond what you see and touch. You should know this by now, though. I have said it often enough. Avoid the institutions of those who swear to know how to build. To create a building requires you to be hands-on. To have stood in the rain, hurriedly trying to protect your work with sheets of hessian and tarp slapping ragged in the driving wind. Having to stop what you love, because of dust in the eye or exhaustion in your body. The talk of wise sages, deemed too common or unclean to sit in the traditional seats of learning, yet who provide wise, salt-of-the-earth dialect worth millions. The pride of real creation emanating from perfect joint and plumbness. If you do not know these things and more, then you are not a builder, nor will you be until you understand such matters. Even one who knows such arts can fail. When the economic god mixes himself into every atom of a building and every thought in its creation, problems will arise and stay. An oak will only grow at the right speed and at the right time. It cannot and will not be hurried. If you hurry it in some way, by genetic manipulation or by other force, then it will suffer and die. As I have said before, economics has marred my passion, twisted my joy and makes me the own despoiler of my work.

As such I am forced to look idle to others in the human

realm. I am reduced to stringing words where I once laid bricks, to carry on my work solely in my mind. I am struggling and for the first time lost. Even my high wisdom is losing its way. I don't know what to do or write or feel. I am rambling through words and life. Sometimes I repeat myself, I know. Now I find myself thinking of glorious days past. And I know that time isn't even real! I sometimes wonder if I am returning to my human self again, if my divine and ancient side is slipping back. My bones remade as they were and my cells made mortal. If he inside me is leaving, then there must be hope, for is he not needed? Or is he leaving a sinking ship with all hope lost? I think that maybe this is a strange time, a time of change and twisted calm and fury. But I will carry on and find what I need again.

13

The main sticking point, you see, is the economic way. When Adam Smith made his enquiry into the wealth of nations, he created a new way of thinking and a change in the policy of governments. The free market has brought wealth and many great things, but is a process that is evolving and has some way to go. Happiness is very slowly being built into the model, but it is the drive for deadlines and speed, time is money, etc, etc. This is what stifles the flow of life.

And so we have arrived at this stage today, where our landscape reflects our lives. Where once every building was as divine as a ziggurat or a pyramid, now they are reduced to a roof over your head over a box. A box that has no depth or life, that isolates you and imprisons you. If you carry on with this, then the emptiness will continue. You smother the land with such structures, stifling the magic that lies beneath them.

I hope you heed my words of wisdom, strung out without

the confidence of my proper craft. I hope you listen and do not see them as entertainment. They are true. This is not fiction, even if they make me sell it as such. My fury and passion are fading, and, although still young, I am tiring and weary. I still have great power, but I lack the will to use it. I sometimes muster the effort to avenge the wronged; I tell you, the wronged, you are not alone. Do not seek revenge. That is for us to carry out by causing regret, redemption and amendment. See the beauty of life and change everything that's wrong. Until you do, I cannot build again, and if I cannot build I cannot live and create this home for you. Your poison poisons my kind. Every hissed breath of wrongdoing and pain is amplified through us. We need all of you as you need us. Remember the power of brevity, remember the embodiment of the brick as a symbol of the human mind and its connection to nature. The power of the smallest and most rejected. The overlooked and most modest is where you will find the best of things. Like me in my shed, made from old doors and battered, rejected timber. Here I carry out a truly priestly act and push every element of me into everything I build. Through every process in creating buildings and life, I live a prayer.

Do the same in your lives. I beg you.

APPENDIX I

His expedition against the Britanni was celebrated for its daring. For he was the first to launch a fleet upon the western ocean and to sail through the Atlantic sea carrying an army to wage war. The island was of incredible magnitude, and furnished much matter of dispute to multitudes of writers, some of whom averred that its name and story had been fabricated, since it never had existed and did not then exist; and in his attempt to occupy it he carried the Roman supremacy beyond the confines of the inhabited world. After twice crossing to the island from the opposite coast of Gaul and in many battles damaging the enemy rather than enriching his own men – for there was nothing worth taking from men who lived in poverty and wretchedness – he brought the war to an end which was not to his liking, it is true; still, he took hostages from the king, imposed tributes, and then sailed away from the island.

Plutarch, *The Life of Julius Caesar*

Carthage, Rome's infamous rival, was at the height of its powers half a millennium before Christ. Around this time a sailor called Himilco set off from Carthage to explore the northern coasts of Europe. He may have followed the trade routes of the Tartessians, a people who lived in what is now modern Andalusia in Spain. He may or may not have been the first, but his journey was apparently fraught with fear, sea monsters and uncertainty. It is possible he came across a fabled island, doubted by many even to exist. He may only have glimpsed the shore through the spray of an angry grey sea, or on a kinder day he may have been able to look closer. He may have seen the occasional figure, or the monuments of a strange and exotic civilisation. We may never know as his journey has become fragmented on the shores of time.

He was, however, followed. Much later, around 325 BC, by a Greek sailor from what is now Marseille who set off to explore the northern reaches of his world. He returned about five years later with tales of the north, including Britain. He said he had travelled widely around the island and wrote a book of his journey: *Peritou Okeanou* (*On the Ocean*). His name was Pytheas.

This book has not survived, but other classical authors were in no doubt aware of it, maybe reading it in full, as they were able to criticise and comment on its contents. It is in the works of these authors that fragments of *On the Ocean* are found.

In his *Natural History* (book IV, chapter 30), Pliny the Elder (AD 23–79) wrote:

Opposite to this coast is the island called Britannia, so celebrated in the records of Greece and of our own country. It is situated to the north-west, and, with a large tract of intervening sea, lies opposite to Germany, Gaul, and Spain, by far the greater part of Europe. Its former name was Albion; but at a later period, all the islands, of which we shall just now briefly make mention, were included under the name of 'Britanniæ' . . . Pytheas and Isidorus say that its circumference is 4,875 miles.

An earlier spelling of 'Britannia' was 'Pretannia', possibly derived from the proto-Celtic language. The people called themselves the 'Pretani' or 'Priteni', 'the people of the forms'. The modern Welsh for Britain is Prydain, hinting at the roots of 'Pretannia'.

So Albion became known as Pretannia, and then Britannia, to the classical world. Pliny's source was not Pytheas' original text. His information came from a now lost work by Timaeus of Tauromenium (*c.*356–*c.*270 BC). Timaeus was a Greek of Sicilian birth, as was Diodorus Siculus (*c.*90–*c.*30 BC). Diodorus also made use of Timaeus in his own work, which he called *Bibliotheca Historica* (*Library of History*). Although he doesn't say so, it seems clear that Diodorus' information about Britain also originated with Pytheas. In book V of *Bibliotheca Historica*, Diodorus says of Britain:

It is triangular in shape, the same as Sicily, but its sides are unequal. Since it extends obliquely from Europe, the headland next the continent, which they call Cantium [Kent], is only about one hundred stadia from the mainland, at which place a strait runs between. A second angle, Belerium by name [the Penwith peninsula of Cornwall], is four days' sail from the continent. The last, called Orca [probably Dunnett Head in Caithness], is said to project out into the sea. The shortest side faces Europe and measures 7,500 stadia; the second, extending from the channel to the extreme north, is said to be 15,000 stadia in length; while the last side measures 20,000 stadia; so the entire circumference of the island is 42,500 stadia. They say that the inhabitants are the original people thereof, and live to this time after their own ancient manner and custom; for in fights they use chariots, as it is said the old Grecian heroes did in the Trojan War. They dwell in simple cottages, usually built of reeds or timbers. In reaping of their corn, they cut off the ears from the stalk, and store them in houses that are roofed over. From thence they take as much of the ripest as will be needed for the day, and after grinding it they prepare their food from it. They are of much sincerity and integrity, far from the craft and knavery of men among us; contented with plain and homely fare, strangers to the excess and luxury of rich men. The island has a large population, and has a cold climate, since it stretches so far to the north, lying directly under the Great Bear. They are governed by several kings and princes, who, for the most part, are at peace and amity one with another. But of their laws, and other things peculiar to this island, we shall treat more particularly when we come to Caesar's expedition into Britain . . .

The material Diodorus is referring to here was either never written or has been lost. He continues:

Now we shall speak something of the tin that is dug and gotten there. They that inhabit the British promontory of Belerium, by reason of their converse with merchants, are more civilised, and courteous to strangers, than the rest are. These are the people that make the tin, which with a great deal of care and labour they dig out of the ground; and that being rocky, the metal is mixed with some veins of earth, out of which they melt the metal, and then refine it; then they beat it into pieces like knuckle-bones, and carry it to a British isle near at hand, called Ictis [possibly Looe Island]. For at low tide, all being dry between them and the island, they convey over in carts a great quantity of tin in the meantime. (There is one thing peculiar to these islands which lie between Britain and Europe: for at full sea, they appear to be islands, but at low water for a long way, they look like so many peninsulas.) Thence the merchants carry into Gaul the tin which they have bought from the inhabitants. And after a journey of thirty days on foot through Gaul, they convey their packs carried by horses to the mouth of the Rhône. But thus much concerning tin.

Julius Caesar tried to invade Britain twice, in 55 BC and 54 BC, and in his accounts we finally have first-hand observations on the British:

The interior of Britain is inhabited by a people who, according to oral tradition – so the Britons themselves say – are aboriginal; the maritime districts by immigrants who crossed over from Belgium to plunder, and attack the aborigines, almost all of them being called after the tribes from whom the first comers were an offshoot. When the war was over they remained in the country and settled down as tillers of the soil. The population is immense: homesteads, closely resembling those of the Gauls, are met with at every turn; and cattle are very numerous. Bronze or gold coins are in use, or, instead of coins, iron bars of fixed weight. Tin is found in the country in the inland, and iron in the maritime districts, but the latter only in small quantities; bronze is imported. Trees exist of all the varieties which occur in Gaul, except the beech and the fir. Hares, fowls, and geese they think it impious to taste; but they keep them for pastime or amusement. The climate is more equable than in Gaul, the cold being less severe. (*The Gallic War* (*Commentarii de Bello Gallico*), book V, chapter 12.)

Caesar continues:

By far the most civilised of all the natives are the inhabitants of Kent – a purely maritime district – whose culture does not differ much from that of the Gauls. The people of the interior do not, for the most part, cultivate grain, but live on milk and flesh-meat and clothe themselves with skins. All the Britons, without exception, stain themselves with woad, which produces a blueish tint; and this gives them a wild look in battle. They wear their hair long, and shave the whole of their body except the head and the upper lip. Groups of ten or twelve men have wives in common, brothers generally sharing with each other and fathers with their sons; the offspring of these unions are counted as the children of the man to whose home the mother, as a virgin, was originally taken. (*The Gallic War*, book V, chapter 14.)

Diodorus Siculus describes the apparel of men in Gaul, though it seems clear that his comments could also apply to the southerly parts of Britain at least:

The clothing they wear is striking; shirts which have been dyed and embroidered in varied colours, and breeches, which they call in their tongue *bracae*. They wear striped cloaks, fastened by a buckle on their shoulder, heavy for winter wear and light for summer, in which are set checks, close together and of varied hues. Their defensive arms are a shield, as high as a man, garnished with their own ensigns; some having the figures of animals raised in bronze on them, and these are skilfully worked with an eye not only to beauty but also to protection. On their heads they put bronze helmets, with large pieces of work raised upon them which give an appearance of great size to those who wear them; for they have either horns of the same metal joined to them, or the fore-parts of birds and beasts . . . Some of them wear iron cuirasses, chain-wrought; but others, content with what arms nature affords them, fight naked. (*Bibliotheca Historica*, book V.)

Ironically we would know very little of the Druids if it wasn't for Julius Caesar. His campaigns in Gaul provide us with the earliest accounts:

Everywhere in Gaul two classes only are of any account or enjoy any distinction; for the masses are regarded almost as slaves, never venture to act on their own initiative, and are not admitted to any council . . . One of the two classes consists of the Druids, the other of the Knights. The former officiate at the worship of the gods, regulate sacrifices, private as well as public, and expound questions of religion. Young men resort to them in large numbers for study, and the people hold them in great respect. They are judges in nearly all disputes, whether between tribes or individuals; and when a crime is committed, when a murder takes place, when a dispute arises about inherited property or boundaries, they settle the matter and fix the awards and fines. If any litigant, whether an individual or a tribe, does not abide by their decision, they excommunicate the offender – the heaviest punishment which they can inflict. Persons who are under such a sentence are looked upon as impious monsters: everybody avoids them, everybody shuns their approach and conversation, for fear of incurring pollution; if they appear as plaintiffs, they are denied justice; nor have they any share in the offices of state. The Druids are all under one head, who commands the highest respect among the order. On his death, if any of the rest is of higher standing than his fellows, he takes the vacant place: if there are several on an equality, the question of supremacy is decided by the votes of the Druids, and sometimes actually by force of arms. The Druids hold an annual session on a settled date at a hallowed spot in the country of the Carnutes – the reputed centre of Gaul. All litigants assemble here from all parts and abide by their decisions and awards. Their doctrine is believed to have been found existing in Britain, and thence to have been imported into Gaul; and nowadays most people who wish to acquire a thorough knowledge of it go there [to Britain] to study. (*The Gallic War*, book 6, chapter 13)

The Druids, as a rule, take no part in war, and do not pay taxes conjointly with other people: they enjoy exemption from military service and immunity from all burdens. Attracted by these great privileges, many persons voluntarily come to learn from them, while many are sent by their parents and relatives. (*The Gallic War*, book 6, chapter 14)

Caesar is, of course, writing from first-hand experience, but it would appear, from a comparison with the writings of Diodorus Siculus and Strabo, that he has simplified the structure of the Gallic learned/priestly class, using 'Druid' as an umbrella term. Strabo, in *Geography* (book IV, chapter 4), says:

Among all the Gallic peoples, generally speaking, there are three sets of men who are held in exceptional honour: the Bards, the Vates and the Druids. The Bards are singers and poets; the Vates, diviners and natural philosophers; while the Druids, in addition to natural philosophy, study also moral philosophy. The Druids are considered the most just of men, and on this account they are entrusted with the decision, not only of the private disputes, but of the public disputes as well; so that, in former times, they even arbitrated cases of war and made the opponents stop when they were about to line up for battle, and the murder cases, in particular, had been turned over to them for decision. Further, when there is a big yield from these cases, there is forthcoming a big yield from the land too, as they think. However, not only the Druids, but others as well, say that men's souls, and also the universe, are indestructible, although both fire and water will at some time or other prevail over them. (Ceaser continues, *The Gallic War*, book 6, chapter 14)

During their novitiate it is said that they learn by heart a great number of verses; and accordingly some remain twenty years in a state of pupillage. It is against the principles of the Druids to commit their doctrines to writing, though, for most other purposes, such as public and private documents, they use Greek characters. Their motive, I take it, is twofold: they are unwilling to allow their doctrine to become common property, or their disciples to trust to documents and neglect to cultivate their memories; for most people find that, if they rely upon documents, they become less diligent in study and their memory is weakened. The doctrine which they are most earnest in inculcating is that the soul does not perish, but that after death it passes from one body to another: this belief they regard as a powerful incentive to valour, as it inspires a contempt for death. They also hold long discussions about the heavenly bodies and their motions, the size of the universe and of the earth, the origin of all things, the power of the gods and the limits of their dominion, and instruct their young scholars accordingly.

The second of the two classes consists of the Knights. On occasion, when war breaks out, as happened almost every year before Caesar's arrival, the Knights either attacking or repelling attack, they all take to the field, and surround themselves with as many armed servants and retainers as their birth and resources permit. This is the only mark of influence and power which they recognise. (*The Gallic War*, book 6, chapter 15)

The Gallic people, in general, are remarkably addicted to religious observances; and for this reason persons suffering from serious maladies and those whose lives are passed in battle and danger offer or vow to offer human sacrifices, and employ the Druids to perform the sacrificial rites; for they believe that unless for man's life the life of man be duly offered, the divine spirit cannot be propitiated. They also hold regular state sacrifices of the same kind. They have, besides, colossal images, the limbs of which, made of wickerwork, they fill with living men and set on fire; and the victims perish, encompassed by the flames. They regard it as more acceptable to the gods to punish those who are caught in the commission of theft, robbery, or any other crime; but, in default of criminals, they actually resort to the sacrifice of the innocent. (*The Gallic War*, book 6, chapter 16)

Diodorus Siculus and Strabo echo Caesar in asserting that it was the Druids who oversaw sacrifices, but they add that observations of a sacrificial victim's death throes were used for divination. However, whilst Diodorus reckoned that the deathblow was a knife thrust above the midriff, Strabo says it was a sword blow to the back. Stabo continues:

We are told of still other kinds of human sacrifices; for example, they would shoot victims to death with arrows, or impale them in the temples, or, having devised a colossus of straw and wood, throw into the colossus cattle and wild animals of all sorts and human beings, and then make a burnt-offering of the whole thing. (*Geography*, book IV, chapter 4.)

The god whom they most reverence is Mercury, whose images abound. He is regarded as the inventor of all arts and the pioneer and guide of travellers; and he is believed to be all-powerful in promoting commerce and the acquisition of wealth. Next to him they reverence Apollo, Mars, Jupiter, and Minerva. Their notions about these deities are much the same as those of other peoples: Apollo they regard as the dispeller of disease, Minerva as the originator of industries and handicrafts, Jupiter as the suzerain of the celestials, and Mars as the lord of war. To Mars, when they have resolved upon battle, they commonly dedicate the spoils: after victory they sacrifice the captured cattle, and collect the rest of the booty in one spot. In the territories of many tribes are to be seen heaps of such spoils reared on consecrated ground; and it has rarely happened that anyone dared, despite religion, either to conceal what he had captured or to remove what had been consecrated. For such an offence the law prescribes the heaviest punishment with torture. (Julius Ceasar, *The Gallic War*, book 6, chapter 17)

When Caesar writes of Mercury, Apollo, etc., he is Romanising the actual names of the native deities, selecting the nearest equivalent from the Roman pantheon of gods. Incidentally, Caesar notes in *The Gallic War* (book VI, chapter 21) that, in contrast, the Germans 'have no Druids to preside over public worship and care nothing for sacrifices. The only deities whom they recognise are those whom they can see, and from whose power they derive manifest benefit, namely, Sun, Moon, and Fire: the rest they have not even heard of.' Of the Gauls he writes:

The Gauls universally describe themselves as descendants of Dis Pater, affirming that this is the Druidical tradition. For this reason they measure all periods of time not by days but by nights, and reckon birthdays, the first of the month, and the first of the year on the principle that day comes after night. As regards the other customs of daily life, about the only point in which they differ from the rest of mankind is this – they do not allow their children to come near them openly until they are old enough for military service; and they regard it as unbecoming for a son, while he is still a boy, to appear in public where his father can see him. (*The Gallic War*, book 6, chapter 18)

It is the custom for married men to take from their own property an amount equivalent, according to valuation, to the sum which they have received from their wives as dowry, and lump the two together. The whole property is jointly administered and the interest saved; and the joint shares of husband and wife, with the interest of past years, go to the survivor. Husbands have power of life and death over their wives as well as their children: on the death of the head of a family of high birth, his relations assemble, and, if his death gives rise to suspicion, examine his wives under torture, like slaves, and, if their guilt is proved, burn them to death with all kinds of tortures. Funerals, considering the Gallic standard of living, are splendid and costly: everything, even including animals, which the departed are supposed to have cared for when they were alive, is consigned to the flames; and shortly before our time slaves and retainers who were known to have been beloved by their masters were burned along with them after the conclusion of the regular obsequies. (*The Gallic War*, book 6, chapters 13–19.)

Perhaps not everything that Caesar says about Gallic customs is relevant to the British, but what he says about Druidism is, presumably, relevant to Britain – Druidism's supposed birth-place. Similarly relevant is the following note, made by Pliny the Elder in his *Natural History*, concerning mistletoe:

Upon this occasion we must not omit to mention the admiration that is lavished upon this plant by the Gauls. The Druids – for that is the name they give to their magicians – held nothing more sacred than the mistletoe and the tree that bears it, supposing always that tree to be the robur [common oak]. Of itself the robur is selected by them to form whole groves, and they perform none of their religious rites without employing branches of it; so much so, that it is very probable that the priests themselves may have received their name from the Greek name for that tree . . .

'*Drus*' is the Greek for 'oak tree'. The meaning and deriva-tion of the word 'Druid' is still the subject of conjecture. The modern English word derives from the Latin '*druides*', which was itself considered by ancient Roman writers to come from the native Celtic Gaulish word for these figures. Other Roman texts also employ the form '*druidae*', while the Greeks used the term '*druids*'. Although no Romano-Celtic word is known, the old Irish '*druî*' ('druid', 'sorcerer') and early Welsh '*dryw*' ('seer') show a link back to these times. By conjecture, a proto-Celtic word may possibly be '*dru-wid-s*' (pl. '*druwides*'), meaning 'oak-knower'. This in turn can go back to the proto-Indo-European roots '*deru-*' and '*weid-*', 'to see'. The modern Irish word for 'oak' is '*dara*', Anglicised in placenames such as Derry, and also Kildare, or 'church of oak'.

Pliny continues on the subject of Druids and oak trees:

In fact, it is the notion with them that everything that grows on it has been sent immediately from heaven, and that the mistletoe upon it is a proof that the tree has been selected by God himself as an object of his especial favour. The mistletoe, however, is but rarely found upon the robur; and when found, is gathered with rites replete with religious awe. This is done more particularly on the sixth day of the moon, the day which is the beginning of their months and years, as also of their ages [i.e. timekeeping cycles], which, with them, are but thirty years. This day they select because the moon, though not yet in the middle of her course, has already considerable power and influence; and they call her by a name which signifies, in their language, the all-healing. Having made all due preparation for the sacrifice and a banquet beneath the trees, they bring thither two white bulls, the horns of which are bound then for the first time. Clad in a white robe the priest ascends the tree, and cuts the mistletoe with a golden sickle, which is received by others in a white cloak. They then immolate the victims, offering up their prayers that God will render this gift of his propitious to those to whom he has so granted it. It is the belief with them that the mistletoe, taken in drink, will impart fecundity to all animals that are barren, and that it is an antidote for all poisons. Such are the religious feelings which we find entertained towards trifling objects among nearly all nations. (*Natural History*, book XVI, chapter 95.)

The only druid from antiquity known by name is Diviciacus or Divitiacus of the Aedui, a people who lived between the Saône and the Loire in what is now France. (He is not to be confused with the king of the Suessiones also known by the Latinised name Diviciacus.) The name means 'avenger'.

The time of his birth is a mystery, but Diviciacus was a man in the late 60s BC, and a senator of the Aedui. He escaped a massacre by the forces of the Sequani, Arverni and Germanic troops under the Suebian leader Ariovistus. Pro Roman, he supported the alliance between the Aedui and Rome. In 63 BC he spoke before the Roman Senate to ask for military aid. While in Rome, he was a guest of Cicero. Julius Caesar, who knew him well, speaks of him several times in his *The Gallic War*, noting his diplomatic skills. Diviciacus' brother, Dumnorix, whose name may mean 'King of the World', however, was passionately against Rome. Dumnorix was executed on the orders of Caesar and it is said that at the end he shouted: 'I am a free man and a citizen of a free state.' The date of Diviciacus' death is unknown, but Cicero speaks of him in the past tense in 44 BC.

In book 1:41 of *On Divination*, Cicero speaks of Diviciacus and other diviners in the world:

And this kind of divination has not been neglected even by barbarian nations; for the Druids in Gaul are diviners, among whom I myself have been acquainted with Divitiacus Aeduus, your own friend and panegyrist, who pretends to the science of nature which the Greeks call physiology, and who asserts that, partly by auguries and partly by conjecture, he foresees future events. Among the Persians they have augurs and diviners, called magi, who at certain seasons all assemble in a temple for mutual conference and consultation; as your college also used to do on the nones of the month. And no man can become a king of Persia who is not previously initiated in the doctrine of the magi.

There are even whole families and nations devoted to divination. The entire city of Telmessus in Caria is such. Likewise in Elis, a city of Peloponnesus, there are two families, called Iamidae and Clutidae, distinguished for their proficiency in divination. And in Syria the Chaldeans have become famous for their astrological predictions, and the subtlety of their genius. Etruria is especially famous for possessing an intimate acquaintance with omens connected with thunderbolts and things of that kind, and the art of explaining the signification of prodigies and portents. This is the reason why our ancestors, during the flourishing days of the empire, enacted that six of the children of the principal senators should be sent, one to each of the Etrurian tribes, to be instructed in the divination of the Etrurians, in order that the science of divination, so intimately connected with religion, might not, owing to the poverty of its professors, be cultivated for merely mercenary motives, and falsified by bribery. The Phrygians, the Pisidians, the Cilicians, and Arabians are accustomed to regulate many of their affairs by the omens which they derive from birds. And the Umbrians do the same, according to report.

Around a hundred years after Julius Caesar last set foot in Britain the Druids made a last stand on the island of Anglesey, as described by Tacitus (AD *c.*55–*c.*117) in *Annals* (book XIV, chapter 30):

On the shore stood the opposing army with its dense array of armed warriors, while between the ranks dashed women, in black attire like the Furies, with hair dishevelled, waving brands. All around, the Druids, lifting up their hands to heaven, and pouring forth dreadful imprecations, scared our soldiers by the unfamiliar sight, so that, as if their limbs were paralysed, they stood motionless, and exposed to wounds. Then urged by their general's appeals and mutual encouragements not to quail before a troop of frenzied women, they bore the standards onwards, smote down all resistance, and wrapped the foe in the flames of his own brands. A force was next set over the conquered, and their groves, devoted to inhuman superstitions, were destroyed. They deemed it indeed a duty to cover their altars with the blood of captives and to consult their deities through human entrails.

Gaius Suetonius Paulinus, the commander sent to subdue Anglesey, could not consolidate his victory, however. Boudicca began her rebellion at the other side of the country and drew him away.

Bear in mind the words above are from the viewpoint of Rome. The real question we should ask is, why has the perspective of the Druids been lost? Why do we find it a mystery, and why write off their ways as backward superstition? After all, the most pragmatic and powerful empire the world had seen seemed to fear them greatly.

Man and woman once roamed the earth free. They understood the nature of life and their indestructible bond with it. They hunted and gathered for their needs. Maybe they gardened and began to cultivate cereals on a small scale. Over the face of the earth they migrated and families united to become tribes. Sometime later, through the growth of populations or the change in climate or geography or even through catastrophe, some people began to turn their gardens into farms. No longer needing to roam, they settled. Life now became a burden. In fact it was harder work than the life of the hunter. Villages formed and communities gathered at regular times for ceremony and trade.

In some parts of the world the gathering places became settled permanently and consortia formed to order the chaos of the marketplace. These consortia evolved and society began to stratify. The generalist became the specialist, trading skills and surrendering an element of freedom. This freedom was passed up through the strata of society and aggregated into the top tier. Somewhere in this process the external freedom of man, his outer life, is divided from his inner freedom. King and priest now have growing portions of his power.

The city creates a surplus of food and now can dominate the region. The surplus can be traded in volumes never seen before, creating a want for exotic items. Goods are replaced by money, part of the evolution of writing. Knowledge is also monetised by writing and the power of memory is long eroded. People very slowly begin to lose the distinction between information and knowledge.

The trade routes of the world are vast and connect the entire world. Ideas flow along them and the introduction of the city-state of mind reaches people everywhere, subtly influencing even isolated lives.

This could be the birth of what philosophers call *materialism.* Materialism holds that the only thing that exists is matter and that the phenomena of nature, including consciousness, are nothing more than an interaction of matter. Think that philosophy is arcane or has little influence on the world now and you would be wrong. Science, with all of its lofty aims to seek the truth, is firmly in the grip of materialism. Work in physics seems to be prising this apart, but the very language of mathematics curtails attempts to escape the restrictions of materialism.

In the millennium before Christ a series of revolutions began to concuss civilisations. This was termed the 'Axial Age' by Karl Jaspers, the German psychiatrist and philosopher. Over generations, an epigenetic frustration with materialism erupted and a new intellectual elite emerged, seeking to reconstruct the world.

For the ancient Britons the links between our earthly existence and the world of the gods were strong, even in synergy. In fact the barriers we now perceive between heaven and earth only began in the Axial Age. The distance between the spirit and the physical world widened. Man cried out, trying to meet very real spiritual needs. A new arbitrariness of life pierced agonisingly deep. Salvation had to arrive or mankind's flame would snuff itself out from within.

The deepest thinkers sought to bridge this gap, through a form of spiritual reason. Questioning the order of things, and rising from a chaotic collection of political and non-political groups, they emerged to form a new intellectual elite. They sought to reorder the world according to a transcendental vision. This vision reordered societies, changing the ways that people related to each other. As the world of prehistory began to fade into what we now perceive as distant and dreamlike, the beginnings of history as we understand it today emerged. Consciousness changed forever.

Independent from the rest of their societies, these thinkers competed even with their own kings for the control and dissemination of the language of God. They formed distinct groups with strata of power. The higher echelons of the groups would hold more knowledge. The larger centres of these ideals would show their power in the production of art, architecture and writing. They would seek to pull in the smaller centres of tradition at their peripheries.

The evolution of these institutions would erode the power of the king, no longer god-like. God was now firmly in the grip of these institutions and the king was now accountable to God or the gods. The life of Caesar shows this struggle beautifully: his belief in his god-like status, and the differing opinion of the Senate.

Continuous reordering of societies and entire civilisations took place throughout the world. This was caused by the very institutionalisation of a believed tension between the orders of heaven and the orders of earth. A continuing cycle of wisdom, revelation and doubt. Buddhism emerged from Hinduism and Christianity from Judaism, just two examples of the revolutions that took place seeking this reordering and reconnection.

Mystical and esoteric traditions arose, trying to resolve this tension between the two worlds.

The counter-philosophy to materialism is idealism. In fact it is said that all philosophers fall into one or other category. Idealism holds that the spirit or the mind comes before matter, even acting on matter. The subject of matter is common to both philosophies as a focus on the nature of reality. The great challenge of mankind now is to form a bridge between these two philosophies. The nature of reality is more nuanced than can be perceived as a single truth. A war for our consciousness rages around us to this day. Axial Age-type tensions are now emerging.

Utopian visions proved the fact that the original needs of revolutions had not been met, a harking back but with the urge to further reorder the world into heaven on earth. An intensity of proselytising zeal to reconstruct the world took hold. From this, intolerant dogma arose. Official, powerful orthodoxies arise.

The orthodox gave rise to the heterodox. This conflict is a defining feature of human history continuing to this day. All views circulate in the hurricane of materialism. A massive amount of energy is required to break free from the whirlwind.

Institutions emerge from collective human will and begin to develop as a thoughtform, independent of the will of their creators. Materialism is the institution we have created and with it we have unleashed a monster. This sums up the true history of Rome.

Caesar wrote that banishment was the greatest punishment for the Gauls, and it could be said that Rome's fear of destruction was the grounding for its zealous quest for survival and conquest.

Emotions are our framework for consciousness. They are the hues with which we sense the world. The Druids understood this and their purpose was to guide humanity through its emotions, towards a mysterious goal.

So it came to be that one of the world's most successful city-states came into contact with Britain, an island protected from the most damaging effects of materialism by the Druids. This was a society that may in effect be the model of an advanced society of the future, existing without a nation state, yet able to defend itself. But materialism had crept across the sea, long before Caesar. The institutionalisation of materialism was foolishly met with the institutionalisation of idealism and the power of the Druids ebbed away.

The Roman contact with Britain is perhaps the most crucial element in this philosophical war, for it was from Britain that the ideals of Rome, still wrestling with the ancient British consciousness, would take firm hold in the world. It continues today predominantly through America.

Gnaeus Julius Agricola was a Roman general who played a large part in the conquest of Britain in AD 43. His son-in-law Tacitus wrote of him in his first published work, *The Agricola*. In it he describes the sorry end of the freedom of man and the arrival of a new consciousness:

The following winter passed without disturbance, and was employed in salutary measures. For, to accustom to rest and repose through the charms of luxury a population scattered and barbarous and therefore inclined to war, Agricola gave private encouragement and public aid to the building of temples, courts of justice and dwelling-houses, praising the energetic, and reproving the indolent. Thus an honourable rivalry took the place of compulsion. He likewise provided a liberal education for the sons of the chiefs, and showed such a preference for the natural powers of the Britons over the industry of the Gauls that they who lately disdained the tongue of Rome now coveted its eloquence. Hence, too, a liking sprang up for our style of dress, and the 'toga' became fashionable. Step by step they were led to things which dispose to vice, the lounge, the bath, the elegant banquet. All this in their ignorance they called civilisation, when it was but a part of their servitude.

APPENDIX 2

Columbkille cecinit while passing alone; and it will be a protection to the person who will repeat it going on a journey.

Alone am I in the mountain,
O royal Sun of prosperous path,
Nothing is to be feared by me,
Nor if I were attended by sixty hundred.

If I were attended by sixty hundred
Of forces, though they would defend the skin,
When once the fixed period of my death arrives
There is no fortress, which will resist it.

Though even in a church the reprobates are slain,
Though in an island in the middle of a lake,
The fortunate of this life are protected,
While in the very front of a battle.

Leon Jenner

No one can slay me
Though he should find me in danger,
Neither can I be protected
The day my life comes to its destined period.

My Life!
Let it be as is pleasing to my God,
Nothing of it shall be wanting,
Addition to it will not be.

The healthy person becomes sick,
The sickly person becomes sound,
The unhappy person gets into order,
The happy person gets into disorder.

Whatever God has destined for one
He goes not from this world until he meets it,
Though a prince should seek more,
The size of a mite he shall not obtain.

A guard
One may bring with him on his path,
But what protection, what
Has guarded him from death?

Bricks

An herb is cut for the kine
After their coming from the mountain;
What induces the owner of the kine
Not to cut an herb for himself?

No son of a man doth know
For whom he maketh a gathering,
Whether it is a gathering for himself
Or a gathering for another person.

Leave out penury for a time,
Attend to hospitality, it is better for thee,
The son of Mary will prosper thee;
Each guest comes to his share.

It is often
The thing which is spent returns,
And the thing which is not spent,
Although it is not spent, it vanishes.

O living God!
Alas for him who doth evil for any thing;
The thing which one sees not cometh to him,
And the thing which he sees vanisheth from his hand.

Leon Jenner

It is not with the sreod our destiny is,
Nor with the bird on the top of the twig,
Nor with the trunk of a knotty tree,
Nor with a sordan hand in hand;
Better is HE in whom we trust,
The Father, the One, and the Son.

The distribution for each evening in the house of God,
It is what my King hath made;
He is the King who made our bodies,
Who will not let me go to-night without aught.

I adore not the voice of birds,
Nor the sreod, nor a destiny on the earthly world,
Nor a son, nor chance, nor woman,
My Druid is Christ, the Son of God,-

Christ, the son of Mary, the great Abbot,
The Father, the Son, and the Holy Spirit.-
My estates are with the King of kings,
My order is at Cenannus and Moen.

Attributed to St Columba, 'The Song of Trust'

Time is made by our consciousness. A reduction of the mysteries of nature so that we can comprehend.

A quantum of reality, bite-sized chunks of the universe are shown to us one at a time. Like the passage of earth through a worm, we take the next bite before the last has passed through, and in this way perceive the forward passage of time.

As this quantum pulse builds matter, and because the next flash comes before the last has faded, a sense of permanence arises and memory gives us the forms that are the basis of our consciousness.

Form is the clothing of energy, where the tailor is time.

Where else better to read this language of forms than in the landscape of 'The People of the Forms'?

Form need not belong to a physical object. It may be attributed to a thought or representation of a thought, such as a word.

The most fascinating words are the words with longevity. Seemingly so perfect that, like a shark or a crocodile they have flowed through time without much of the friction of evolution. Unlike the words '*sreod*' and '*sordan*', whose meanings are now lost, such a word is '*coombe*'. Both this word and the feature it describes form part of the steganography of the Druids.

A coombe is the end of a dry valley. The word 'coombe' comes from Brythonic, the language of the Druids. It means 'hollow'. If you were to take a map and look at, for example, the South Downs, you would find many features with 'Coombe' in their name. Around them would be monuments such as causewayed enclosures, barrows and maybe even standing stones – connected by some of the most well-trodden paths in the world.

But these man-made features, the visible and the lost, which hold such fascination are nowhere near as sacred as the coombe. Invariably filled with hidden archaeology from the flint man to the Roman and beyond, the coombe is the most important and sacred of sites.

Made by the power of nature through the mystery of time, the coombe seems as if it was placed there by our consciousness before we even arrived. On the barren winter day when the icy wind cuts through, the coombe is silent, windless and calm. A house in a coombe could last a thousand years, its people even longer. Part of an ancient landscape once filled with people and now empty and dry as it ever has been.

The towns now loom around, pushing the people from the land. But a deep bond with the landscape, made over many millennia, seems to flow like mist and sit in these valleys. Time whispers from these places and so do the Druids.

Their knowledge hidden in plain sight.